VETERANS CRISIS HOTLINE

VETERANS CRISIS HOTLINE

JON CHOPAN

University of Massachusetts Press
Amherst and Boston

This book is the winner of the 2017 Gracy Paley Prize in Short Fiction. The Association of Writers & Writing Programs, which sponsors the award, is a national nonprofit organization dedicated to serving American letters, writers, and programs of writing. Its headquarters are at George Mason University, Fairfax, Virginia, and its website is www.awpwriter.org.

ISBN 978-1-62534-368-0 (hardcover)

Designed by Sally Nichols
Set in Adobe Garamond Pro and Treadstone Grunge

Cover design by Kristina Kachele Design, llc
Cover photo by Faberr Ink/Shutterstock.com.

Library of Congress Cataloging-in-Publication Data
Names: Chopan, Jon, author.
Title: Veterans crisis hotline / Jon Chopan.
Description: Amherst and Boston : University of Massachusetts Press, [2018] |
    Series: Grace Paley Prize in Short Fiction |
Identifiers: LCCN 2018019139 (print) | LCCN 2018021532 (ebook) | ISBN
    9781613766149 (e-book) | ISBN 9781613766156 (e-book) | ISBN
    9781625343680 (hardcover)
Classification: LCC PS3603.H667 (ebook) | LCC PS3603.H667 A6 2018
    (print) | DDC 813/.6—dc23
LC record available at https://lccn.loc.gov/2018019139

British Library Cataloguing-in-Publication Data
A catalog record for this book is available from the British Library.

These stories have appeared, in slightly different form, in the following publications: "The Cumulative Effect" in *Post Road* and *Redux;* "Men of Principle" in *Epiphany* and *Home of the Brave: Somewhere in the Sand;* "A Full and Happy Life" in *The Adirondack Review;* "Battle Buddy" in *Drunken Boat;* "On Leave" (as "Homecoming") in *Em;* "Valor" in *decomP;* "On the Euphrates," in *Boiler;* "Bullet Catcher" in *Southampton Review;* "AWOL" in *Consequence;* "Slaughter" in *Glimmer Train;* "Rules of Engagement" in *Blood Orange Review;* and "Crisis Hotline: Veterans Press 1" in *Hotel Amerika.* Quote used as epigraph from *The Things They Carried* by Tim O'Brien. Copyright © 1990 by Tim O'Brien. Reprinted by permission of Houghton Mifflin Harcourt Publishing Company. All rights reserved.

For Nick and David,
who were willing to share their stories with me

It was very sad, he thought. The things men carried inside. The things men did or felt they had to do.

—Tim O'Brien, "The Things They Carried"

CONTENTS

ACKNOWLEDGMENTS

I am indebted to my colleagues at Eckerd College, especially K. C. Wolfe and Scott Ward. They have always supported my work and believed in it. This is true, too, of Ira Sukrungruang, who has always been the best mentor and friend an artist could have.

Special thanks go to AWP and the University of Massachusetts Press for giving me this opportunity. Thanks also go to Sue Miller for pulling my manuscript out of the pile and finding some good in it.

I am grateful to so many people: my mother, Joan, has always given me a shoulder to cry on; my father, Steve, has always had stories and humor to offer; my brother, Jeff, is there whenever the chips are down and knows how to be a big little brother; Dan Gervais read every story and poked holes in them all and always asked when he was going to see new work. Thanks most of all to Christina Lutz, who nurtured me and my writing, who was unafraid to say the hard things, who knew the outer edges of my talents and always, always pressed me to reach them and to push beyond.

VETERANS
CRISIS
HOTLINE

CRISIS HOTLINE
VETERANS PRESS 1

Sometimes, when they call the hotline, they want to talk to another vet. They ask for us specifically. They have this perception that only those who've seen war can understand the suffering born of it. As far as I can tell, this is a myth. It is, to my mind, like asking the criminally insane to cure one another.

I started working at the Veterans Crisis Line around Christmas. This was a few months after we began sending bombing raids into Syria to fight ISIS. The phones rang nonstop, what with the holidays and the news that another war was, more or less, starting up. By then, I'd dealt with my own issues, had come home, drank, fought, fucked, called the hotline a handful of times, sought treatment at the VA, and finally landed this gig. The worst of it was behind me. I was sure of that much.

But some nights the snow piled so high and so fast, encased the whole city in a stunning white coffin, a place where there was nothing else to do but curl up and dream about the past.

I had, for some time, avoided veterans. I took the job because my friends and doctors thought it would do me good, helping other guys who were struggling with the things I'd struggled with. Everyone thought it would be good for me, listening to other men confess.

Not everyone who called the hotline was looking to kill themselves or even thinking about it. Some were old widowers. Some were lonely bachelors who were looking for dating advice. Others were fine, except that they needed an audience to tell a war story to, someone who'd yet to hear it. Reliving it gave them a sort of pleasure, or maybe catharsis. One man who was in his nineties called me every week. Each time he called he asked for me by name, caught me up on the news from his neighborhood, "current events" he called it. Mostly it was gossip about the young soccer mom next door, the cheating husband. He talked about them so much that I felt like they had become characters in my own life. He was a veteran of the Second World War, but he never talked to me about that.

I did this full time, four days on and three days off. The idea was that the stress of it might get to us, so we got those three days to kind of decompress, but I missed it when I wasn't working. We were there to keep guys from killing themselves, but I found myself talking a lot and it felt good. We weren't supposed to do much of that, get personal with callers, become friends, for obvious reason. But I took it personally when the same grunt called three shifts in a row, saying, "This time I'm going to do it. This time it's for real." I held the phone away from my ear to keep from screaming. I could still hear him, his labored breathing, "Hello? Hello?" he said. So many of them were like that, desperate to hear a voice on the other end of the line. It wasn't that they wanted to be told no, it was that they wanted someone's company, didn't want to die alone. I have no doubt that the men who called, looking to take their own lives, meant it. I could see them, huddled in the dark, because I had been one of them.

There were others, like this one guy who'd suffered some sort of brain injury, something that affected his short-term memory. He would walk from one room to the next never knowing why he'd traveled from point A to point B. All he had were those old memories. There was no future for him beyond the age of twenty-one, or no future that he would someday see as a past. He couldn't remember the last time he'd fucked, what he'd eaten for breakfast that morning. How could he, he wondered, go on living like that, with no recollection, with nothing but the years before his injury and the very moment he was in?

What could I say to that, except that there were a lot of things he'd be better off forgetting, that he had a pretty good excuse to get away with all kinds of bullshit. In the end, I offered, what was the point in living any life if you didn't realize that the whole thing was one big joke? At least he'd found his punch line.

There were, of course, the types you hear about on the news. Men with amputations. Men who held onto memories of the dead, both friend and foe. Those who could not make sense of anything they'd seen or done. I'm ashamed to admit that I've forgotten most of them now. It isn't their condition that's made me forget, so much as the fact that there was nothing funny about them.

★ ★ ★

The building we worked in was on the very outskirts of greater Rochester, surrounded by cows and fields of corn. There was a VA clinic on one side of us and a horse track on the other, places where veterans would come to seek treatment or entertainment. None of them were aware of the fact that we were huddled inside the building in between, the place many of them called when they returned home late at night. I knew these men because there was a shuttle that brought them out here from the surrounding areas. I rode it back and forth from Rochester each day, where I was staying with a nurse who worked at the local clinic there, who was taking care of me on her own time. Each night, I'd stare off into the surrounding fields as we traveled the Thruway in the dark, snow falling softly outside, the silence of lonely men humming inside. Often, I felt a great wave of calm pour over me as I boarded the bus, thinking about all that silence, knowing that no one would call on me to speak, to save them. The winter days were cold and dark, but I felt most at home as we barreled down the road, a kind of piecemeal platoon.

★ ★ ★

Early in my time at the hotline, I saw them loading an amputee onto the bus as I approached. He sat there smiling, as the lift slowly raised him up, snow sticking to his hair and piling on top of his head. I could see him sitting at home later, with the phone pressed to his ear, telling someone at the call center about how humiliating it was, sitting there like that, the other veterans lined up and waiting for him before they could board themselves. No one said anything, of course, but I felt humiliated for him, though he seemed fine, unaffected, and unashamed.

On the bus, he sat alone in the back in a space designed for his wheelchair. The bus driver buckled it into place and pulled a seat belt around the man, checking with him to make sure it was just right, making sure he was comfortable.

I thought I might sit in the aisle across from him and try to start a conversation, see how he'd come by his injuries. For some reason I cannot describe, he fascinated me. He didn't seem at all fazed by his condition.

I sat huddled against the window watching his reflection so that I didn't have to stare directly at him. Everyone else faced forward and stayed quiet. He disappeared and reappeared as we went through pockets of light. I looked over a few times to make sure he was still there, that his chair hadn't moved, which was something I worried about. He'd started humming, a tune so soft and low that I couldn't make it out. He was wearing cammies that were cut off around the thigh, and a little bit of his leg stuck out on each side. The skin appeared rough and chewed on in places. He looked out his window. I worried that he would notice my reflection, see that I was studying him, but I didn't know where else to look and didn't know what to say to him. I felt foolish, but I couldn't stop myself from wondering why he seemed so happy, why it was that there was nothing about him that hinted at surrender.

When we reached the parking lot he sat patiently while the others filed out. He looked over and winked at me, as if he knew the whole time what I'd been thinking. I wanted to apologize, offer to help him off the bus. But I didn't know the first thing about how to help and thought he might take offense if I offered and then turned out to be of no use.

The woman I was staying with wouldn't be off for another hour. I could see inside the clinic, the local news playing on the TV in the lobby, the sad faces of the men who sat waiting, and I thought, I can't go in there, I can't be near them right now. I hadn't felt this way in a long time. Usually I went in, talked with them, and stayed warm while she finished up. But that day, I was repulsed by the very idea.

That whole time, the man in the wheelchair and the bus driver had been going about the business of getting off the bus. I hadn't even realized it. All of a sudden, I had an overwhelming urge to talk to this man, afraid that I might not get another chance. I scrambled toward the door just as the bus driver was fastening the man onto the lift.

"Hey, partner," the man in the chair said, "we thought you were asleep with your eyes open."

"Figured we'd let you dream a bit longer," the driver said.

I blinked a few times, trying to remember if I'd been sleeping. "Do you need any help?" I said.

"No, we're good," said the man in the chair.

Once he was lowered down, I got off the bus and we shared a smoke. I told him I didn't want to go inside and asked if he'd keep me company while I waited. It had stopped snowing by then. We were huddled under an awning in the back of the building where the nurses took cigarette breaks. "Sure," he said, "Who'd want to sit with that crowd anyhow?"

★ ★ ★

This woman I was seeing, the nurse, we'd met during one of my initial trips to the clinic in Rochester, which mostly dealt with physical ailments, by which I mean colds, sore throats, diarrhea. For serious stuff they sent you to Buffalo where they kept the surgeons and psychologists. For physical therapy or chronic pain they sent you out to the clinic next to the hotline. The Rochester clinic was a way station on the road to the required treatment. This nurse was going to medical school to become a doctor at the University of Rochester and worked at the VA as a part of her training, or something like that. She was not a veteran and, as far as I knew, I was the only veteran in her life.

The strange thing about our relationship, at the time, was that it wasn't physical, which only seems strange to me now because she was beautiful and I was very attracted to her. Mostly we sat around and watched old movies, ate takeout, and always she wanted to talk about the war. She was the first person I really talked to about stuff like that. She had eyes that were sort of uniquely shaped, because her father was German and her mother was Korean. They were this shade of brown that reminded me of a very deep river, the kind of eyes that made you want to tell a person something of consequence, maybe something you'd never tell another person. I thought, when it first started, that this relationship wasn't going to be romantic because she had her life together and I was hardly holding on. But, late at night, when she grew tired, she'd fall asleep on my arm, and one morning she'd asked me why I didn't try anything while she was asleep. She seemed to believe that I was some kind of monster waiting for my chance to take advantage of her. She told me she knew that I was going to hurt her, but that it wouldn't surprise her and therefore wasn't a big deal. I thought to ask her what made her think of me that way, thought that maybe it had to do with my being a marine, with the things I'd told her. But I knew that, in all likelihood, it had very little to do with me and more likely had something to do with her past. I wanted to ask her about that, but somehow I knew that I wasn't supposed to, knew that if she told me, she'd stop letting me come around, would stop falling asleep next to me each night, which, for a while, was the only real pleasure I knew and so didn't have the courage to risk losing.

That's how it went. I'd wait for her after work each night, we'd go home together and fall asleep on the couch, me afraid to move for fear she'd wake, her waiting for me to hurt her.

I came and went as I pleased, but whenever I returned, she let me in without question. She wasn't worried about where I'd been or who I'd been with. Instead, we spent time catching up about what was going on with her schooling, what was new at the hotline. I mostly stuck to the good stuff, by which I mean happy. I didn't talk to her about the hard parts of the job, the men who killed themselves while I was on the line, waiting while the police and ambulance crews sped through the night. She was going to be a good doctor, I could tell. She remembered every one of her patients, the specific details of their aliments, yes, but also the things about them that made them unique. I like to think we shared that. I like to remember that time with her as good for both of us. There was, after all, a great deal of pain stored up inside of her, and it seemed to me that she only knew joy through taking care of others.

★ ★ ★

By February, I'd become friends with the man in the wheel-chair, Eddie. Often we'd catch a cab from the clinic and go out drinking together before making our way to his house for a nightcap.

I began splitting my time evenly between Eddie and the nurse. When I told her about Eddie, she asked me why I was spending so much time with him. It wasn't said in judgment or with jealousy, she was only curious. But I couldn't answer her then. I'm not sure I could even now.

Being with Eddie, listening to him talk about the war, his life, the way he seemed, unlike so many of us, happy: all of that drew me to him. But there was something else, something about the way he interacted with the men at the bar. He treated me, though he was only a few years older, like a son.

One of the more fascinating aspects about Eddie was his refusal to use prosthetics, which his family and doctors had been trying to push on him since he'd arrived home. He believed that there was no shame in being without his legs, that he didn't need to fix anything about himself. I respected that, though I guessed that there was more to it.

Usually we drank at a bar called Four Brothers, a sad little joint on the east side of town occupied by a handful of regulars, old men who came together for a few hours before returning home to their loneliness. There was nothing special about them, this small group of men who talked about sports and politics and the way this country had changed. But there was a kind of happiness about them, a sort of energy that filled those few hours spent talking in the dimly lit bar with other men. Very rarely were there any women or newcomers. Only this same group, slowly sipping at their beers and laughing as the darkness outside grew thick and the air grew cold.

I didn't think I belonged with them. But Eddie, the youngest one other than me, seemed right at home. He told stories. Joked. I could imagine him spending the rest of his life there, not worried about the present, the future, the past. I sat in silence, listening to everything he said, waiting for some sign, a hint of his unhappiness. I had yet to see the differences between diseases of the body and diseases of the mind.

It was a night like this, after we'd arrived at Eddie's house, when he asked me to touch his legs. Mostly when we drank we had only a few pitchers before wandering out into the night for one final drink at Eddie's. Then I would catch a cab to my parents' place, where I had a key, and I would sleep in the basement, eating breakfast with them in the morning before heading back to the call center. That night, after our normal glass of whiskey, Eddie asked me to stay and have another.

"We've never gotten really drunk together, Byrne," he said. "Let's get drunk."

"What's the occasion?" I asked.

He hesitated for a moment, refilling both our glasses. I suspected that there were many things he wanted to say. During our time together, Eddie hadn't spoken much about lovers, friends, old military buddies. Perhaps, I thought, he was feeling especially lonely that night.

"It seems like a good night," he said.

We drank recklessly, which was something I hadn't done in a long time. But in the safety of Eddie's house, it didn't seem like all the other times. At some point we sat next to one another, watching snow fall outside the living room window. We hadn't slept, and I watched the first plumes of light coming up over the city. Eddie was wearing only a pair of underwear, so that his bare legs stuck out, ending somewhere just after the edge of the couch. I'd looked down at them a few times over the course of the night, but now, in my exhaustion, I stared at them.

"Go ahead and touch one," Eddie said.

"What's that?" I said, looking away, trying to pretend that I hadn't been staring.

"There's nothing to feel guilty about, Byrne."

I sat up then, feeling exhausted but also exhilarated. I wanted to touch them, to see what the mangled flesh felt like. I looked at him.

"It's okay," he said.

I scooted to the edge of my seat and bent forward, resting my hands on my knees, before moving my right hand, very slowly, toward Eddie. I did touch his wounds, I am sure of that. But what I remember now, very vividly, is my hand frozen between us, shaking with anticipation, and Eddie leaning back, Eddie closing his eyes.

★ ★ ★

On Sundays, I went to a local AA meeting at a Baptist church near Four Brothers. Often I did this right before meeting Eddie for drinks. I went because there was something especially familiar about these people, and because I had the luxury of being the only veteran. Had there been another, I'm sure I wouldn't have continued to go.

"Sometimes, when I'm walking about, feeling sorry for myself," the leader of the group said, a man who'd tried to corner me on more than one occasion to talk to me about my drinking, "I think about other people and how their suffering is so much greater than mine. You know? People who've suffered some kind of violence or lost loved ones to it, people who are disabled or dying from some incurable disease. But, I must remind myself, I too have a disease." He often said things like this, especially after I told one of my war stories, which were the only stories I told and had nothing to do with drinking but had the effect of making everyone very supportive of me.

I sat there, thinking about the men who called the hotline, about Eddie. Who knew why some of us were diseased and others weren't? Much as we wanted to believe it, there didn't seem to be any reason for it.

★ ★ ★

For a little while, I lost track of Eddie. He'd stopped riding the bus because he'd completed his intensive physical therapy and only needed to go to the local clinic for checkups. On my end, I'd started staying later at the clinic, picking up extra shifts, drifting home on the last bus, where I would fall asleep and dream about doing it all over again.

Near the end of that fall and the beginning of winter, I received a call from Eddie. We had not, in a good stretch of time, seen one another. I was fully committed to my new life and, I hate to admit this now, I'd left Eddie behind. He asked me to come to his place, said he'd consider it a real favor. I wouldn't say he begged, but there was a great deal of urgency in his voice. I could tell that he needed me to do this for him. For a few seconds, the line went silent and I looked out at the first flakes of snow. I felt, despite the brevity of our time together, like I owed him this. But I didn't want to go. I'd grown comfortable with my new life, comfortable dealing with other people's suffering from a distance like I did at the hotline. I didn't want to see it up close anymore.

When Eddie opened the door it was clear he was sick, and bad. He was sweating and shivering. His hair matted to his head. He was covered in layers of clothing. I could see that he hadn't showered in days, maybe even a week. The room smelled of his sickness.

"Jesus," I said. "Why haven't you been to the clinic?"

He wheeled away from the door and toward his bedroom. "I thought it'd get better. Thought it was just a bad cold."

"Do you want me to take you?" I said.

Eddie stopped at the door to his room. "I need you to help me first."

His apartment was sweltering. He must have turned the heat up to eighty-five degrees.

"Whatever I can do."

He went into his room. I followed. He sat by the door to the bathroom. The fifty feet he'd traveled looked to have exhausted him.

"I can't go there like this," he said. He turned his head and looked toward the bathroom, the tub, but he didn't say the words.

For a moment, we both looked in on it, neither of us saying

anything. I could've told him that a bath didn't matter, that getting to the clinic was the most important thing. I saw, for the first time, that it was not that he didn't have shame. Of course he did, as we all do. But what I was finally seeing was his pride, which was the opposite of shame, a will to go on living like the rest of us despite his condition.

I walked past him and began running the water, testing it with my hand for a few seconds before turning to undress him. He closed his eyes as I pulled the layers away and folded them in a neat pile, which I set on the edge of his bed. When he was down to his underwear, I wheeled him into the room and closed the door behind us. I'm not sure why I did that, except that it felt like this was a private thing, something that required the outside world to be completely shut out.

I waited for the tub to be full before I removed his underwear and lifted his naked body from his chair. He wrapped his arm around my neck, and despite his sickness I could feel how strong he was. For the first time, his strength was apparent to me.

This whole time his eyes remained closed and he was silent. He was shivering, but he held on tightly as I gently bent to lower him into the water. I thought to leave him then, to let him clean himself, but I didn't think I could bear to wait for him, not inside his house, not after having come this far.

As I kneeled down on the floor, taking a bar of soap into a washcloth, Eddie began weeping very quietly. He opened his eyes briefly to make sure, I think, that I was still there. Then he leaned back and wept openly.

There were other sounds, too, coming from other parts of the apartment complex: music, running water, a hissing sound emitting from the ancient radiator. I took the cloth and began washing Eddie's neck, scrubbing him softly. The water was very warm and his body smelled of ammonia. There was steam rising from the tub, rising from his body.

At some point, not long after I started, Eddie reached up and took my hand. He held it, gently, for a time. I thought I should say something to him then, comfort him, but I didn't know what I could say that would make him feel better, and I wasn't sure he wanted that anyway.

Later, they would diagnose him with pneumonia. He would recover, of course. He was young and strong and had a great desire to live. I'd learned that much in my time with him. But there, in his dimly lit bathroom, as I scrubbed him and rinsed him clean, as I put shampoo in his hair and gently poured water over his head, he wept and I said nothing, knowing, finally, that this was the only comfort he would ever ask of me.

★ ★ ★

By this time, things with the nurse were different; I'd started staying with her for longer stretches. We spent our days together walking in the younger neighborhoods, Park Ave., where college kids and newlyweds lived, went to the nice bars and restaurants, museums. At some point, without our noticing, things had changed.

One night, shortly after I'd went to see Eddie, she told me about her secret, the thing I suspected she'd been keeping to herself. She'd been raped in her first year of medical school, had gotten pregnant, and had had an abortion. Until she met me, she had avoided men. She'd let me in because she knew I was damaged, in my own way, and she'd finally accepted me when she saw that I was just a driveling thing who needed someone to love me, someone who would not make me talk about it anymore. She believed, long before I did, that I was getting better, that I would turn out all right.

The winter was just starting up and I was staying with her every night, sleeping in on the weekends, sitting together on the couch quietly in the mornings. I always woke before her and walked to a little shop nearby where I got us pastries and coffee. When I returned, I'd leaf through her textbooks while she enjoyed the last bit of her dreams. I had no delusions about becoming a doctor, but I wanted to understand her world, wanted to know the language, even if I could never speak it. When we sat together, she didn't need me to tell her about the past anymore. She didn't need me to say anything. And the longer this went on, the stronger I felt, the more certain I was that I was prepared for a normal life, where the things of the past were just that and not some kind of vision I was running toward or away from.

It was a winter morning like this when we slept together for the first time. She came into the living room, covered in the residue of sleep, and took me into the bedroom. The first thing I noticed was that the blinds were wide open, that sunlight poured in and covered everything. I thought, there is nowhere to hide a secret in a place like this, nowhere to hide any ugliness.

Then she laid me in bed and undressed me and sat over me, looking into my eyes. I'd never been with a woman like this, all that light and her looking right at me. It was not a thing I was used to. It was something new and strange to me, being seen and seeing someone, looking at them and knowing that there was nowhere you might run to.

This was how it went. Always in the morning, the light streaming in, looking at one another. And after a while I could not imagine ever doing it again in any other way.

In her bed, afterward, she rested with her head on my chest and I talked. Dust and daylight poured over us. The future stood before us, the past a thing that we might let go. I could see it, this future, and I told her so. Children, maybe. Travel. Lost days, holed up inside, not talking, dreaming. Maybe we'd move away when she was done with medical school, find a place without snow. Maybe we could start our lives together away from the dark, cold place where we'd found one another. But she said she'd never ask me to leave, knew how much I needed the hotline, needed to talk to those lonely men on the edge of death. When I told her that it was just a job, that I could live without it, she said that we both knew it was a lot more than that and that maybe I couldn't.

* * *

I keep a list of the men who have taken their lives while I am on the phone with them. When I receive a call I go through a series of predetermined questions. Are you alone? Do you have a weapon? Have you been drinking? In most cases, they are alone, they do have a weapon, and they have been drinking, but I ask anyways to get the conversation started and to ease into it. You don't want to start with an explosive thing like, why do you want to kill yourself? That only stands to escalate the situation. After that, I ask if they'll put down the weapon while we talk. And then, regardless of how that goes,

I'm more or less off script, improvising my way through on a case-by-case basis. While all this happens, as I begin to accumulate details, assess the seriousness of the situation, I am in contact with another member of the hotline team via instant messaging. They're there to call local police and ambulance personnel in case things take a turn, which doesn't always mean suicide, but means that things are pointed in that direction.

I am not a religious man, have never believed in the power of confession. But there I was, the most violent and secret parts of my life behind me, a vast and indefinite future before me, listening to men tell me their stories, believing that I might, just for listening, save them.

VALOR

Name: Thomas ████████
Service: Army
Tour Dates: ████████████
Location: Chicago, IL
Duration: 06:00.14

'd just laid down for my first nap in forty-eight hours when another firefight broke out. We were living in a civilian home, a one-room flat, that the army was renting from an Iraqi citizen.

Brandon Pettit was next to me, on his hands and knees, blood on his fingers, his white t-shirt covered in dirt, a pair of cooking tongs hanging out of his pocket. He was smoking a cigarette.

"What's going on?" I said.

Pettit sat down, pulling the tongs from his pocket. "Styza's been shot."

"Is he dead?"

"No, just blind is all."

I sat up, saw Styza laid out on the floor. He wasn't making any noise. "He looks dead."

"I'm fine," Styza said. "But I can't see shit."

Pettit slid forward, leaned toward Styza's face with the oversized tweezers. "This is gonna hurt," he said.

One week before this, our medic had been wounded by an IED, and now Pettit, a community college dropout, the only one among us to have taken any science since high school, was playing doctor until the new guy arrived. He insisted we call him Doc. "I've earned it," he said with a smile.

Just then the firefight ended, as they so often did, without reason or redress. The rest of our fire team sat around in a circle starring at the grotesque scene before us.

"What happened?" I asked.

"He stuck his head out the window and caught one between the eyes," Watkins said.

Pettit stared into Styza's face. He ran his forearm over his own sweaty forehead. "Fuck," he said.

"What's the matter?" Styza said.

"I can't do it, man," Pettit said. "I can't pull the thing out."

"Just do it, pussy," Styza said.

I was confused. "You aren't trying to remove that thing, are you?"

"It was his idea," Watkins said, pointing at Styza.

"I'd do it myself," Styza said, "but my arms are numb."

On the other side of Styza a whole set of medical devices and products had been spread out. There were gauze and rubbing alcohol and scissors, tubes of morphine, two or three of them uncapped and ready to go.

"You got a better idea?" Styza said.

"Did you give him morphine?" I asked Pettit.

"Not yet. I didn't know how much he needed."

"It doesn't hurt," Styza said,

"That's a good sign," Watkins said.

Pettit handed me the tongs, reached over Styza and grabbed a wad of gauze. "You pull it out, Mulley," he said, "I'll stop the bleeding."

"I'm not touching him," I said.

Styza said, "Somebody better do something. One of you assholes better do something."

"Not me," Watkins said.

"Well, I'm not," Pettit said.

Styza held his hand up, weakly, "Somebody light me a cigarette."

"I'm on that," Watkins said.

"We could draw straws?" Pettit offered.

"Should we drive him to the nearest post?" I said, "Let their doc handle it?"

"Sure," Styza said, "If Doctor Pettit don't mind calling for a consultation."

"What do you think?" I said.

"Okay, I guess," Pettit said.

"We'll tell him you done all you could," I said, trying to reassure him. "We'll tell him you recommend removing the bullet."

I stood over Styza for the first time. The bullet looked like the ass of a worm stuck in a rotting apple. No one was especially fond of the guy, but none of us wanted him to die either. I grabbed his arms and Pettit stood, grabbing his feet.

We laid Styza across the backseat of the Humvee, and the three of us, Styza and Pettit and I, took off.

★ ★ ★

A few weeks before, Styza had shot a civilian, and ever since we'd been coming under daily fire. We blamed him for the suffering we endured, Pettit especially, because they'd never gotten along. Styza picked on him, called him names, belittled Pettit every chance he got. For some reason, a reason only Styza knew, he hated Pettit from the first time they met.

We zoomed forward down a dusty road that ran along the Euphrates. I did my best to hit every pothole I could.

Pettit picked up the radio and said, "Breaker, breaker, one, nine."

"What are you trying to do?" I asked.

"Alpha, Beta, Omega. This is Tango, Tango, Tango. Over." Styza stretched across the backseat moaning as if he were a child trying to get someone's attention.

Pettit played with the dials on the radio, and I heard the faint sound of static like fireworks fizzling out in the sky.

"How you holding up back there?" I asked Styza.

"I think my vision is coming back," he said, wiggling his fingers in front of his face.

Before us stood a long stretch of flat land that looked like the carcass of an abandoned lake. It was as if God had sucked every ounce of juice from the earth. The sand was sawdust. The heat seeped from the earth in waves. We moved forward but nothing came closer.

There were buzzards circling high in the air above us, and below there were dead things waiting to be eaten. Pettit put the radio down and pulled a pack of Camels from one of his pockets. He held a cigarette in one hand and let the other dip in and out of the breeze. He seemed happy to be there.

"We might win a medal for this," he said.

"I doubt that," I said.

I could hear Styza mumbling something beneath his breath, which gave me comfort, because the kid was never quiet, and I was certain that the only way anyone would ever be sure he was dead was if he shut his mouth.

"You'd nominate us for a medal, wouldn't you?"

"Why are you asking me?" I said.

"I'm asking him," Pettit said, gesturing with his cigarette toward Styza.

Suddenly Styza sat up, pressing his head between us. "I got it," he said.

"Fuck," Pettit said.

Blood was running down Styza's face and getting on everything.

Pettit looked at me, and I could see that he'd gone white.

"What'd you do that for?" I said.

"It feels better, I think. My eyes are working again. I can see light. It's not all dark like it was before."

"Fuck," Pettit said, again.

"Calm down," I said.

"He's gonna die now for sure."

"He's not gonna die," I said, but there was a lot of blood and Styza had already fallen back, slumped against the seats.

Pettit's idea, about receiving those medals, had gotten stuck in my head. The army loved to shower people with awards for all the regular shit, common valor they'd called it. But this was something different, something bigger somehow.

"Don't die until we get there," I told Styza. "At least you could do us that one favor."

Pettit said, "He doesn't look so hot."

But Styza survived, though he never regained his vision, and Pettit and I did receive medals for valor, Bronze Stars. Of course, we didn't know any of that yet.

Pettit looked back at Styza, who was passed out and bleeding everywhere, and then turned and looked at me. "I think I'm gonna be a doctor," he said. "Someday."

There we were in the cradle of civilization. If I believed in God I might have thought that there was something profound about what was happening to us. I might have thought that this was some sign about justice and karma and the failed war effort. But I didn't. There'd been war in that part of the world for centuries, and any hope for peace had been abandoned. No one was waiting for a savior. No one had any illusions about salvation.

MEN OF PRINCIPLE

Name: Matt ███████
Service: Marine Corps
Tour Dates: ████████████████
Location: Rochester, NY
Duration: 15:42.60

I found the guy I was looking for at Six Pockets. I was with my two buddies, Lesh and Jeff. The night before, Clara, the woman I'd just started seeing, had told me about a guy who raped her years ago. I was sure I knew him, though by the time I started looking I'd forgotten his name and was, with foggy recollection, searching for a face. I'd been back from the war for three months by then. The celebration was over, most of the questions about combat had been asked, all of my stories had been told, and I was, just then, becoming accustomed to home life, the drinking, seeing a woman with some regularity, a shit job at the meat-packing plant. In many ways, I was a civilian. But I had not forgotten things about the war—a desire for swift justice, for example. How sometimes, when a guy from our division was hurt or killed, be it by sniper fire or an IED, we'd walk the streets and harass civilians. Or, if we were in a remote location, how we'd stand, circling an empty mosque, and fire round after round until the building was nothing but pockmarked cement. In this way, what we sought was often the quick and necessary relief men feel when they feel loss. It seemed to me then that I was just a young man and could not access a language for my pain and so released it through force. But it occurs to me now that this is too often something that affects all men. From a young age we are taught that to feel anything is to be weak.

That night we started at the Mirage. I was looking for the guy everywhere. I wanted to find him because of what Clara had told me. I thought I could, through an act of violence, even the score. I had told my friends I was looking for him, but not why, told them I was sure I'd seen the guy a week or two before, maybe at the Mirage, maybe at Six Pockets. I wanted to find him and I wanted their help, because, as memory served, he was a big guy, the type of guy who would require strength I didn't have.

When we arrived at the strip club, I was too distracted to "participate in the festivities," as Lesh called them. Every time the front door swung open a gust of cold January air punched into the room, and I turned trying to make out the face, which appeared to be illuminated in the contrast between the light of the outside and the dark of the inside. The Mirage was a strange kind of place. On the edge of the working-class neighborhoods of Lake Avenue and set in the middle of the Kodak industrial park, it attracted an odd mix of blue- and white-collar men. This, somehow, made the place feel even more remote, even more artificial than the average strip club. They catered to both sets of regulars: domestic beer and strange imports none of us drank, the skinny college girls who danced every other set and then the "full-figured girls," as Jeff said. All I knew, when I was there, was that I never wanted anything in my real life to feel as fake as the inside of that place. In part, this was why I drank so recklessly, but also, because I could not calm my nerves, tapped my foot rapidly and out of pace with the music just to keep myself in my seat. I had, to that point, sounded two false alarms. My friends were growing tired of me.

"Look at these fucking broads," Lesh said.

We sat close to the stage, drinking Genny Light and eating twenty-five-cent wings. Jeff stood up during every song and tipped each girl a dollar.

"The fuck you doing that for?" Lesh asked Jeff when he sat down again.

"What?"

"You don't have to tip all of them for every goddamned song," Lesh said. "You're setting an awfully high standard for the rest of us. You're making the ugly ones think it's all right they're ugly."

The girl on stage stopped dancing and shot Lesh a glance. He was a scrawny guy, wiry arms and legs, with stubble on his face at all times. It was hard to decide at any given moment, because of the look of him, whether he'd had a particularly good or a particularly bad day.

"I didn't mean you, honey, you're fine." He licked wing sauce off his fingers, pulled money from his wallet.

"Somebody's gotta make up for Foley," Jeff said, pointing to me, because I didn't get near the stage, did everything in my power, even on a normal night, to divert my attention, staring into the bottom of a beer, watching whatever game was on the televisions tucked in the far corners.

Just then the door swung open and another man walked in. I turned and stared.

"Remind me why you're looking for this guy?" Jeff said.

"Long story," I said. "Just have to sort something out."

Jeff finished off a wing. He washed it down with half a beer. "Relax," he said. "You're starting to creep me out. We're bound to run into him sooner or later."

I refilled my glass, looked up at the stage where Lesh was talking to the girl he'd offended.

We had come to the Mirage, in part, because of my search, but more importantly we'd come because this was one of Lesh's spots, one of the places on Friday and Saturday nights where he sold cocaine. He brought Jeff and me along as a kind of protection. He didn't believe in guns, but felt strongly about a show of force. Jeff was six-foot-four, a bulky 280 pounds. He walked with the long slow strides of a caveman, his arms hung by his sides as if he were carrying clubs in each hand. He was all the force one coke dealer needed, or at least that's what I thought. But Lesh said he liked using my credentials. "United States Marine," he said. "Pretty badass."

The song ended and Jeff moved to get up. He liked the next girl, was bound, at some point, to get a lap dance from her.

"I just want to find this guy and settle it," I said.

"Foley, enjoy the show," he said. "I'm trying to, but you're making it awfully fucking hard."

I laughed.

"What?" he said, reaching into his pockets for his wad of singles.

"That was a pun," I said.

Jeff finished off the other half of his beer.

"See?" he said. "Your head's in the wrong place."

★ ★ ★

Because Lesh dealt coke, we had what could be called special privileges. During a lull the DJ waved us over. My friends rose in unison. Our time to move, make the deal, and head out for a few more, before ending the night at Six Pockets, where Lesh held court, met with regulars, often disappeared into the backroom with the owner or one of the bartenders.

Just then the door opened again and I turned to look. The place was getting packed because some college football team was playing a big bowl game and it was cold and no one wanted to drive home in this weather.

"Jesus," Lesh said. "This shit again."

I stayed in my seat. I wanted to make sure it wasn't him. It was getting dark out so it was harder to make out the faces. I could see snow falling in the background, coming down in sheets that looked like laundry twisting in the breeze on a clothesline.

"You coming, or what?" Jeff asked.

"Yeah," I said, standing up.

Jeff smiled. We were headed into the dressing room, which was his favorite part. "Jesus, man, you really know how to ruin a good time," he said.

We walked, Lesh in front, me in the middle, Jeff in back. When we got to the curtain the DJ parted it. "Gentlemen," he said. We stopped a few steps in so Lesh could make nice with the owner.

"Paradise," Jeff said.

The backroom at the Mirage looked like a locker room, each girl with her own stall, some with makeup strewn about, others with wigs hanging in tangled piles. Behind them, in a corner, were a set of beds where the girls would lie, resting between sets, catching up on sleep they had not gotten between their day jobs and this. All of them seemed more beautiful than they had on stage. They wore bathrobes, smelled of too-sweet perfume, let their hair fall around their shoulders and down their backs.

The girls moved around us with the pace and force of fish trapped in a net. A woman just like them came over to us, started talking to Lesh. She was tall, with dark hair, and she looked too pretty, somehow, to be here. By the way she spoke I imagined her as someone older, like the mother of all the girls there. But she couldn't, by the look of her, have been. She reminded me of Clara. Something about how out of place she seemed, something about the confidence she exuded. It was what had drawn me to Clara, made me believe that she could save me from the world I had come from, was surrounded by at that very moment.

This woman, she looked over Lesh's shoulder at me. "What's wrong with that one?" she said.

Lesh turned toward me. "The smaller one?" he said.

"Yes."

He smiled, turning back to her. "He's just shy is all."

Before long the whole thing was over and my friends were sitting in a circle with some of the girls, a pile of coke in the middle of them, enjoying a few lines before we moved on to our next stop. I sat by myself, thinking about what I would do if I found the guy I was looking for, trying to decide what I'd say to him. The woman who reminded me of Clara walked up to me then, smiling, and put her hand out.

"Can I do something for you?" she said.

I felt very sad just then. Somehow everything felt cheaper. My head was cloudy from all the beer I'd drunk.

"No thanks," I said, my arms folded across my chest.

She untied the belt on her robe.

"What's the problem?" she said, her hands on her hips.

She looked very young then, younger than I'd guessed before. It was because she was so thin, too thin really, with her long hair framing her, and her eyes a blue something like lake water.

"Not you," I said. "I'm with someone."

She leaned in then, her robe falling away. She put her mouth on mine, ran her tongue over my lips. I closed my eyes. The music from the front room hit its peak, the men whistling and cheering for the girl who was dancing. I kept spinning. I inhaled deep gusts of perfume. I was so overcome with grief I thought it might suffocate me. And then she stood, pulled her robe tight, winked at me.

"I love men of principle," she said.

★ ★ ★

On the way to Six Pockets, we made a pit stop. By then I was pretty drunk and needed the break. We drove through the city, across town, toward the low rises and split-level houses of the projects. In the summer months these neighborhoods would be swarming with people, with life, but in January they looked abandoned, picked over, with a few lights on here and there. The roads were slick and lightly dusted in a fine snow that kept falling, but mostly just swirled in tornado-like cyclones, stirred by the winter wind. The building we stopped in front of, a three-story brick apartment complex, looked ready to sink into the earth beneath it. It was dark with the exception of the flickers of candlelit shadows moving behind the static of snow.

As we climbed the stairs to the third floor, I felt a sensation I'd felt when I was as at war, going to a specific target to inspect a house, a feeling that this was not a place where good things happened. The door to the apartment looked worse off than any of the others, the screen hanging from the bottom hinge, slumped over, open, resting against the rail. Lesh walked right in.

Over his shoulder I could see that the room was lit with giant candles resting on sheets of tinfoil, probably purchased in bulk at the public market. The room was heated by a single space heater and I could see my breath in the air. I heard the faint cries of an infant somewhere in the next room.

Once inside I plopped myself into a worn-out Barcalounger, ready, I was certain, to sleep and dream forever. Jeff sat on the couch next to the man we'd come to see and Lesh stood over a plastic table, the kind people might use for picnics or weekly card games. He opened a bag and laid out a line. A woman stood in the doorway between this room and the next.

"Your buddy all right?" the man said, pointing over to me.

"Yeah," Lesh said. "He's a marine; he's just being all inconspicuous and shit."

The man laughed. I flashed them a thumbs-up. Jeff sat with his hands in his pockets, watching the woman as she paced.

"Hey, you want a line?" the man asked, motioning toward me.

I shifted my weight, slid down the chair a bit so my head was the only thing touching the back. "No thanks," I said. "Not my cup of tea." In this room I felt thirsty. I could taste some kind of cruelty that both intrigued and repulsed me, the trace of a perfume that could destroy everything.

"I see," he said. He walked over to the table and blew a line. "A regular G. I. Joe," he said. "A real boy scout." He laughed. I smiled.

Before I knew what was happening Lesh had him pinned to the floor, his hand around his throat. "What'd you say, you idiot, what'd you say to my friend?"

The baby was crying in the next room. The woman made a move toward Lesh, but he held his hand up, palm open. "You're gonna make it worse," he said. She stood, frozen. I sat upright, awake again. The woman glanced at Jeff, then at me. She looked like a child who knew a beating was coming, wanted us to do something to stop it. She knew her husband, or boyfriend, whatever he was, was in trouble, but she didn't know how to save him and neither did we.

The room was quiet except for the sound of the child. I wondered if it was a boy or a girl. I wondered how old it was. The man put his hands around Lesh's. I could see he was having a hard time breathing. I could see he was trying to say something.

"Apologize," Lesh said. "Apologize for what you said."

The baby kept crying. And I felt like we, all of us in that

room, in that part of the city, that we were living hollowed-out lives, like bone with no marrow.

★ ★ ★

On the way to Six Pockets I told them, repeated Clara's story exactly as she'd told it to me. In that instant I could see their faces change, the way it often happens when men are given a real purpose, a mission to believe in. It was as though, suddenly, nothing we'd done that night had ever even happened, like we'd, the three of us, been born again to bring justice to an unjust world.

As soon as we walked through the door I spotted him. A song by Jimi Hendrix was playing, a tune I knew but couldn't place. I elbowed Lesh. "That's the guy," I said. "That's him."

We walked over to the bar. Lesh made small talk with the bartender, ordered all of us drinks. "That's him," he said, elbowing Jeff, pointing right at him.

Six Pockets was only half full, mainly regulars, the drunks on the bar side, the pool leagues finishing up on the other. I couldn't stop looking at the guy, waiting for something to happen, for a chance to arise. He stood by the jukebox with a group of people, his pool team. They were saying their good-byes, readying to leave.

"He's a goddamn monster," Lesh said. "He's bigger than Jeff, for Christ's sake."

"You aren't scared, are you?" Jeff asked, laughing, taking a drink.

The man moved to the bar, his team leaving, sat down and ordered.

I felt, because of all that had happened that night, like I had spent my whole life looking for him, and now that he was alone I wanted to get him outside right away, I wanted to confront him and get it over with.

Lesh finished off his drink. "No. I'm just saying he's big is all."

"Well," Jeff said. "What do you want to do?"

"I'll get him outside," Lesh said. "He's bought shit from me before."

I sat on the stool next to Lesh. Jeff stood behind us. Another Hendrix song came on. People were leaving in small groups. It was settling into a nice slow night, just regulars and the few stragglers from the pool league.

"Then what?" Jeff asked.

"Then," Lesh said, "follow me out. We'll go from there."

★ ★ ★

When we got outside Lesh was talking to him. They were smoking and laughing. The patio was empty, except for the four of us, our arms drawn in toward our bodies, fighting off the cold. Jeff handed me a Marlboro and we stood, the three of us facing the guy, blowing smoke at him.

"My buddy Foley here," Lesh said, "he says he knows you." The laughter had left his voice.

The man looked right at me. Our eyes locked and I could see him searching for me in his memory. Lesh sat down in one of the plastic lawn chairs, put his arms behind his head. Jeff spat on the ground at his feet. The man looked away for a second as a car left the lot, flicked his cigarette into the snow.

"I'm afraid I can't place you," he said, reaching out his hand.

I pulled my cigarette to my mouth, drew in a deep breath. "Well, I know you," I said, exhaling puffs of smoke as I spoke. "I've heard about you."

"Okay," he said.

"I know what you did," I said.

The man pulled his hand back then. "I'm not sure I know what you're talking about," he said. He took a step back. For the first time it dawned on him that we had not come as friends.

He looked at Lesh. "Is this a joke?" he said.

Lesh smiled. "No," he said. "No joke."

"What's up then, what's the problem?"

When I heard him say that, something in me snapped. I guess all along I imagined he'd fess up to it, start bawling like some kid who'd got caught stealing, and, before it even came to violence, he'd fall to his knees and beg our forgiveness. His ignorance made all the anger and disgust I had for him rise up into my throat.

Before I could do anything, Lesh got up and punched the guy in the Adam's apple. The man fell to his knees, and the weight of his falling popped one of his kneecaps free of the socket. Lesh grabbed the lawn chair he'd been sitting on and smashed it over the guy's back, the whole thing splintering into pieces. Lesh stood there with only the arms of it left in his grip.

"That's the fucking problem," Lesh said, tossing the arms aside.

No one said anything after that. All I could hear was that man sucking for air. I brought my knee to his face, could feel his nose bend and snap as he rolled, slowly, like a dog going down to play dead. There was no stopping the beating that followed. We set to kicking him, Jeff stepping back so Lesh and I could work on him uninhibited. We kept at it like we were trying to kick in a door. With each kick a sense of righteousness pulsed through me, something I'd never felt before.

In Iraq nothing seemed this pure, this right. When we moved into cities, when we engaged with the enemy, it always felt played out, because no one really knew who was good and who was bad or why we were even there. The people we fought against hid in plain clothes among the population. Who could blame them, in a sense, because otherwise they had no chance. But then, too, it seemed like a cowardly thing to do. It meant so many people who should not have been killed were. Fighting a war like that had a way of muddying the line between the good guys and the bad guys. It had a way of making things happen that could not be clearly or easily divided into right or wrong. You did, sometimes against your better judgment, anything you could to feel safe, to feel like you'd make it through the war and get home. Because of that, I needed a righteous cause, needed a clearly defined enemy and a valid reason to destroy him.

We were winded after a while. The snow stopped falling and the ground began to freeze. I stood, doubled over, sucking in air that burned my lungs. Lesh lit a cigarette.

"Jesus," Jeff said. "Look at that fucking mess."

In front of us, the man lay curled in the fetal position, writhing, not knowing which parts of him hurt the most. "Shut up," Lesh said, flicking ashes on him. "You're giving me a headache."

I started coughing, violently. My muscles were already getting sore. I picked up my beer, finished what was left.

"Carry him to the bathroom," Lesh said, pointing to Jeff.

"What for?" he asked. "I think you pretty well ruined his night as it is."

I caught my breath, held the empty bottle in my hand. Lesh looked over at me. "Bring that," he said, pointing to it. "We're going to finish this."

★ ★ ★

I held the bottle in my hand. The lights in the bathroom reminded me of the lighting at a police station. I thought of myself, if only for a second, as a cop beating the information out of a suspect. I wanted to say all the cheesy things I thought a TV detective might say, make him confess, make him beg for his life, but I was tired just then, was sick from the whole thing, ready to go back to the bar and drink another beer. I was angry, because what we'd done hadn't fixed anything for Clara, and I knew now, when she found out, that she'd leave me, that she wouldn't find any good in it. I just wanted the guy to disappear.

"You're a piece of shit," I said. "A real piece of shit."

Lesh spat on him. Jeff stood with his back against the door, holding it shut so no one could come in. "Let's get this over with," Lesh said, bending down to get a closer look at the guy. Someone knocked on the door. "Fuck off," Jeff said.

I looked down at the man for a few seconds, sitting there in his own blood, his own piss. I felt sorry for him, but that only made me hate him more. After a minute, I raised the bottle up over my head.

"You've got the wrong guy," he said, spitting out strings of blood. It was something in the sound of his voice, how desperate it was. I knew that he was telling the truth. I knew that he was not the one.

But I said, "I don't care," said, "You're going to pay."

RULES OF ENGAGEMENT

Name: Michael ██████
Service: Army
Tour Dates: ████████████
Location: Tampa, FL
Duration: 07:17.64

was pulling guard duty with a guy named Kyle Rivers, who claimed to be a badass soldier, a real haji killer. As far as I could tell he'd never killed anything, was just some Long Island punk who didn't want to be a yuppie like his parents. I hated the guy. But I'd been paired with him for almost everything to this point and was trying my best to get along with him, or at least tolerate him.

"This war is boring," he said.

"Boring is good," I said.

I believed that, because what sane person wanted that kind of excitement? I'd only joined the army because I didn't have any other options, or nothing that was going to get me out of the shithole I'd been born in.

Rivers leaned into his weapon and scanned the perimeter for movement. He swung around and pointed his rifle at my head.

"See anything worth killing, Rambo?"

"I could end your life right now," he said.

"You're too scared to pull the trigger."

He turned his rifle away, spat out a long trail of tobacco juice near my boot.

I smiled and looked down the road that led to our post.

"You'll see," he said. "I'll kill so many hajis your head'll spin."

"My head'll spin if you kill one."

Rivers stood up, moved closer to me so that I was covered by his shadow.

"You're not as big as I thought you were," I said.

"You keep pushing my buttons," he said, pressing his pelvis against my shoulder, "and I'm gonna fuck you up. Do you understand me? Do you get that?"

I thought about head-butting him in his junk.

"Roger," I said.

"You think you're real funny," he said, "a regular old joker. Mr. Joke Man."

"Everything's serious to me," I said.

He kept standing there. "You'll see."

"What do you want me to say? You're a warrior, a real killer."

"Fuck off," he said, as he sat down, looked away from me.

"I mean it, natural-born killer," I said, patting him on the back, now that I could see how hurt he was.

A few days before, we'd been in a firefight outside Al Asid, a minor skirmish where the enemy fired and we fired back, neither of us hitting anything. Rivers glued himself to a wall and refused to fire his weapon. He claimed he'd been hit. Later, no one could find the wound. I asked him about that, if he was afraid, worried he'd get killed. He walked away from me. I stood, smoking a cigarette, as he wandered off into a small patch of brush, somewhere he wouldn't be seen. I can't be sure, but I thought I heard crying, a soft sad thing, something rising from the bushes. He claimed, later, that he was taking a leak.

We'd been up in the guard tower for two hours when a man approached. He stopped, fifty yards outside the gate, waving an AK and screaming something in Arabic. A voice came over the radio, "Tower, do you have eyes on the man approaching the gate? Do you see a weapon?"

Rivers grabbed at it before I could. "Roger," he said. "We have eyes on the target."

It was a beautiful day, not hot and oppressive like it could be. I was reminded of a resort town, the type of place families might vacation.

I leveled my weapon and examined the man. He was firing random bursts into the air.

"Doesn't look like he's trying to hurt anyone," I said, looking up at Rivers. "Threat level, zero."

"What the fuck are you talking about?" he said.

"Harmless."

"He's firing a weapon," he told me.

I sat back in my chair, placing my hands behind my head. I was thinking about how much time was left before I could go play poker, or jerk off, or grab some food. The thought of killing this man hadn't even crossed my mind.

The radio called in, "Tower, prepare to fire warning shots."

Rivers leveled his weapon. He was shaking so badly that he could hardly hold onto the thing.

"You all right?" I asked.

He looked at me, wiping the sweat from his brow. I could see the frustration building in his forehead, where a purple vein was thickening.

"Breathe," I said.

Rivers lowered his weapon and turned toward me. He looked like he was going to vomit.

"It's okay," I said.

He tried to raise his weapon again, but his hands were all over the place. I thought, because of the way he was positioned, that he was going to fire a round and blow off my head.

I reached over and pushed his rifle toward the floor. "Slow down, killer," I said, "let me handle this part."

I let off a burst ten yards in front of the guy and waited, but he only stopped to reload. A few minutes later another call came over the radio declaring the man a live target, which meant we could go ahead and kill him. Under the rules of engagement a target becomes live after verbal and physical warnings have been ignored.

Rivers sat in his chair trying to get control of his hands. His rifle rested against his knee and he kept talking at it, or to it, I couldn't tell which. He still looked sick. He seemed to be wrestling with something out of reach, slowly realizing that he was being destroyed.

Just then our lieutenant arrived in the tower. He looked at Rivers and then trained his rifle on the target. "What seems to be the problem, gentlemen?" he said, without lowering his weapon.

Rivers said nothing.

I almost felt sorry for him. There was a part of him that was too decent or too scared to do the things war required, and I envied that about him. But mostly I thought it was pathetic.

"Giving our target ample time to retreat," I said.

"If you're joking right now, Harker," the LT said, "I'm not laughing."

By then our shift was half over. I weighed my options now that the LT was there. They seemed limited. I knew that I was going to be the one to do the killing. This was one of those moments when you realize what kinds of awful things you're capable of and how you can do them without regret.

The man stood off in the field, still firing rounds at random things. A rabid dog waiting to be put down. I leveled my weapon.

There were mountains that rose behind him, lush things that I hadn't expected to see in a desert country. The sun hovered just behind them, covering us all in a purple shadow, so that I couldn't see the features of his face. But I could see the shape of him, the size and weight.

I took my time examining him. He was heavyset, I remember that. It surprised me. I thought, perhaps because of the movies, that he would be meek, starved-looking. I didn't imagine why he was this way, if he was, for instance, a middle-aged father. I didn't care who he was or why he was standing in this field. I didn't wish that he had gone away after the warning shots. But I had no real interest in killing him either.

I was not, like Rivers, looking to impress anyone. I knew that killing men was a part of war.

"What's the holdup?" the LT said.

I clicked off my safety and adjusted my aim, but before I could fire Rivers reached for me.

"Wait, Harker," he said, but made no real effort to stop me. He began mumbling, "I can do it. I want to," over and over again.

"No," I said, shaking his hand off of me.

Two men are reborn together, one asking the other for forgiveness. But I couldn't give it. There was no kindness in me. And who am I now? What did I expect I'd become?

"You don't have to do it," he said.

"I do."

"You won't tell the others, will you?"

I looked at the LT, who shook his head and let out a sigh. This whole thing was very pathetic to him.

I leveled my weapon, let out a short burst, and watched the man fall to the ground.

After a minute, the LT said, "First kill?"

"Yes, sir," I said.

He raised his weapon and examined the man I'd shot. I thought, for a second, that maybe I'd only wounded him and raised my weapon to check. He was not moving. If he was alive, he wouldn't be for long.

The LT lowered his weapon and patted me on the back. "Good work, son." He shouldered his rifle and made to leave, but Rivers began crying, real tears, the kind that might come if your girl had just left you, the tears of a man who knew that what he wanted was out there, that he'd never get it back.

We didn't speak for a time.

Later, Rivers told the others that it was buck fever, that he was so excited to get his first kill, so overcome with joy, he said, that he couldn't even aim his weapon. He laughed, but the LT and I, we knew better.

Rivers was still sobbing when I reached over and grabbed his weapon away from him. Some men, they don't have it in them to kill others. That doesn't mean they aren't capable of killing themselves. As I slowly pulled his rifle toward me, he came with it, leaned in so that his head came to rest on my knee. There were tears soaking into my pant leg. I handed the weapon to the LT, who looked at me, his eyes full of genuine disbelief. He left us there, ashamed to watch.

Rivers didn't move from me for some time but instead let out a series of soft moans. It was the kind of noise one might hear coming from a dying animal, worn out and ready to surrender to death. I looked at the mountains as he wept. The sun had sunk behind them and already there were vultures circling in the sky above.

The dead man lay on his back. His giant belly gave him the look of a sleeping drunk. When I've told this story before, people have asked me what I felt, looking down on the first man I'd ever killed. Nothing, I tell them. I felt nothing for him because he was dead. But Rivers, he sat there bawling like a disappointed child, and, though I hated him, I felt very sorry for him. I knew what he felt like, finally knowing who he was.

"It's over," I said softly, once Rivers had gone quiet. I lit a cigarette and began cleaning my weapon, dismantling it piece by piece and putting it back together again. The sound a kind of lullaby.

A FULL AND HAPPY LIFE

Name: David ███████
Service: Marine Corps
Tour Dates: ███████████████
Location: Cleveland, OH
Duration: 11:31.50

One night my buddy Tristan and I decided to check ourselves into the VA hospital in Cleveland for rehab. This was just after one of the guys from Bravo Company killed himself. Tristan thought it was a sign.

"Look, man," he said. "We've had some good times, but I think we ought to get our shit together."

I was twenty-five, a veteran of the Iraq War. I hacked up chunks of phlegm from all the cigarettes I'd already smoked in my life. We sat in Tristan's studio apartment watching *Jeopardy*, screaming out answers while we drank beer and grew more and more intoxicated.

"What is the Civil War?" I said.

Tristan pulled a cigarette from his pack. "Dude, are you even listening to me?"

I took a drink from my beer and leaned back.

Tristan blew smoke toward the ceiling. "The war's over for us," he said. "Time to figure out what we're gonna do next."

I was distracted because it was Final Jeopardy and I had done especially well that night.

"Yeah," I said.

I leaned in and listened for the clue.

"Who is Sir Francis Drake?" I shouted.

Tristan stood and walked over to the TV. He turned it off and then walked back to his seat. He lit another cigarette and softly tossed the lighter at me.

"Bardsley," he said, "What do you want, brother?"

★ ★ ★

In the VA parking lot, we were greeted by protesters who held signs with burnt babies and wounded veterans on them. The president had just announced that we would be in Afghanistan until 2014, and possibly beyond. Fifty thousand troops were still in Iraq.

"When will it end?" they kept chanting, "How long will our nation be at war?"

Tristan and I checked in at the front desk. The nurse came around and drew us a little map, pointed us in the direction of the elevators, said, "You're looking for the psych ward."

When we arrived we were separated. Tristan was going to have special tests run because of the brain injury he'd sustained during his final tour. Later, when he showed up with his head shaved, he told me they'd strapped him to a gurney and performed electroshock therapy on him. He told me they ran a hot soldering iron around in his head, trying to mend the broken connections. I knew he was making it up, but I didn't want to say so and lose him on our first day. Anyhow, sometime later he admitted it.

"That shit before was just a joke," he said. "They shaved me down so they could see inside my head, read my thoughts."

After lunch they gathered us all, the new arrivals, five or six of us. "The class of 2011," one of the orderlies laughed, as they marched us into a conference room to watch a film about what our group sessions should look like. They'd filmed a bunch of guys talking about the moment they knew they'd hit the bottom, about the dumb shit they'd done to ruin their lives. I kept thinking about how pathetic it was to get up there and say that stuff, like crapping your pants in public. I wasn't ready to admit to any of it.

* * *

After the movie I met with my personal counselor, Amanda. She was a beautiful woman in high heels and a skirt. I liked her right away, but that didn't mean I was going to make her life easy.

"Mr. Bardsley," she said, "it's nice to meet you."

"David," I said. "Just call me David."

Her office was full of light and it made her degrees, which hung on the wall behind her, glow.

"Those supposed to prove you can cure me?" I asked her, pointing at them.

She smiled and leaned forward, resting her elbows on her desk. "Is that what you want? Do you want to be cured?"

"Well, I'm here, aren't I?"

She smiled. She'd probably seen this act a few times. Though she looked young in the light of her office, maybe my age, which would mean she was a newly minted doctor or maybe even doing some kind of residency.

"Why are you here, David?" she said.

"The food. I heard the food is pretty killer," I said.

She laughed. "Someone lied to you."

"Figures." I stood up and went to the bookshelves behind me, started running my finger over the spines of all her books. "These come with the office?" I said.

"No, they're mine," she said.

I pulled one of the books off the shelf. It had to do with PTSD, which was all the rage when dealing with vets.

"Why are you really here, David?"

"I already told you, Doc, three square meals."

"You're serious about recovering, aren't you?"

"I'll never drink another drop in my life, Doc, if that's what you want to hear."

"This isn't about what I want, David."

I put the book back. I sat down in my chair again. I couldn't tell her, just then, that I had only come for Tristan. Then she might make me leave, I thought. Then she might want to ask me real questions.

"I'll say whatever you need me to, Doc."

"The truth works."

I leaned forward and smiled. "I told you twice now, Doc," I said. "This isn't going to work if you don't listen to me, now is it?"

* * *

My roommate's name was Ryan Bobbitt. Bobbitt never said a word, was, for all I knew, brain-dead or, at the very least, a deaf mute. Always, during our daily group meetings, Doctor Johnson, the head shrink, would ask Bobbitt a question, as if he might, this time, answer. It was a sad, pathetic thing to watch. Sometimes it seemed like the doc was just teasing Bobbitt, but the truth, as far as I could tell, was that he believed in what he was doing, genuinely felt that he could help even the worst among us, which is why I hated him so much.

We were in our fifth group session when I lost it, when I couldn't take Doc Johnson and his stupid questions anymore.

"Ryan, what's your idea of a full and happy life?" There was a substantial silence.

We sat in a semicircle facing Doc Johnson. Every day we did this, discussing one thing or another, telling stories or even sitting silently. The doc wasn't one to press. Mostly he found ways to coax things out of people.

"What do we think, gentlemen? How would we define a full and happy life? What would we want?"

I snickered, which was my first mistake.

"David," Doc Johnson said, "what do you think?"

I paused for a moment. I had an answer but I was weighing my options. It would have been easy enough, playing this game: money and a beautiful woman, a big house and a white picket fence. I could've said the shit he wanted to hear. Not recovering but faking it.

"I was just thinking that Bobbitt, his wish would be pretty simple."

"How is that?" Doc Johnson said.

"Well, I suppose he'd want his mind back, for starters."

Some of the guys laughed. A few sat there with blank stares.

Tristan tapped me on the knee, whispered, "Go easy, Bardsley. Go easy."

"Well, what about you, David," Doc Johnson said. "Are your wants so different from Mr. Bobbitt's?"

"How could they be the same," I said. "Look at the dude."

Bobbitt sat there drooling on himself and the rest of the guys got quiet. No one was going to join me in my rebellion. No one thought I was being funny anymore. I felt a sudden rush of guilt, a stink that could not be scrubbed away.

"I suppose, in a manner of speaking, there isn't much difference between any of us and Ryan," Doc Johnson said. "We all, it would seem to me, suffer from an inability to speak, at least sometimes."

I could've cried, apologized, like those dudes in the videos we'd watched when we first arrived. I could've fallen to my knees and confessed everything, every nasty minute of my life, every crushing ounce of disappointment and shame and fear. I could have done all that, but instead, without any real provocation, I stood up and knocked my chair back.

"I'm nothing like that fucking retard," I said.

I could see the sadness in Doc Johnson's eyes. He knew he was losing me. I could see his mind working it through, trying to find the one thing he might say to calm me.

"A full and happy life, David," Doc Johnson said. "What is your version of a full and happy life?"

Everyone was watching me to see how I'd handle this.

"A cigarette and a cold beer," I said.

"Is that all you need to be happy?"

I knew that he was trying to work his voodoo now, to get me talking about drinking, which would only lead to me talking about the war and about coming home and about how home wasn't the same anymore, how it wasn't really like being home at all.

I stood there staring at him. I turned to Tristan.

"Let's get out of here," I said.

Tristan looked up at me. I could tell by the way he shook his head just slightly that he didn't want to, that he thought I was making an ass of myself.

Tristan looked over at Doc Johnson and gave him a kind of nod.

"It's your call," Doc Johnson said.

Tristan looked up at me, again. "I'm gonna stay," he said.

I felt betrayed.

"Fine," I said, and now I was beginning to panic. "You stay here with this lifeless pack of fuckups. You go ahead and hold hands and talk about how bad it hurts."

"Come on, man," Tristan said. He reached out for me but I pulled away.

I looked around at the rest of them. They were looking down at the floor, waiting for my outburst to be over.

"What's the matter," I said, talking to Tristan. "You gonna cry like some schoolgirl bitch?"

He didn't say anything. He looked away.

I started walking toward the door. No one was going with me. They were ready to sit in that circle and talk about their drinking and the war, about the lives they saw in their nightmares and the ones they saw in their dreams.

"You dumb motherfuckers," I said. "They can't cure us. There ain't no cure for what we got."

★ ★ ★

It was snowing outside, the thick, wet, lake-effect kind that clings to everything. The protesters were there again. Now they were making snow angels in the parking lot, singing songs about peace and love. I heard the words, but could make nothing of their meaning. Not then, anyhow.

I'd been sober for a shade under a week. I had nowhere to go, so I walked, looking for the nearest bar, thinking maybe I'd have a drink, because it was around four o'clock, which meant happy hour would start soon, somewhere.

The snow was so thick and blinding that I could hardly see my next step, as if God were trying to keep me from the places that felt most familiar to me. Everything vanished. I lurched forward, drawn on by the sound of people's voices calling out to one another. For a few seconds everyone knew the same panic. Down the alleyways and in the streets, I felt the future bearing down on me. Something yet to come. A vision. An inevitability.

The thick powder piled higher and higher as if it might bury us alive. Then, just like that, it stopped. My counselor, Amanda, was up ahead. The snow had lifted just in time for me to see her, but she hadn't seen me, I was certain, so I chased after her.

A few blocks later she entered the city's art museum. I watched her through the glass doors. She took off her coat and smiled at the guard. She walked into the gallery and didn't notice when I followed.

Inside, they were showcasing the work of a mad man named Henry Darger. The attendant let me in for free when I told her I was a vet. There were three rooms with the Darger stuff. His paintings and collages were full of little girls, children, who were at war.

I found Amanda studying a painting in the furthest room over. A group of small girls were surrounding a dragon, trying to bring it to its knees. I wanted to reach across the length of that room and touch her. I wanted to ask her what she saw when she looked into it.

There were a group of people near her, other professional types. A man approached and I heard him say, "You work with the damaged souls over at the VA hospital, don't you?"

"I wouldn't call them that," she said.

"Well, lost souls, then?"

"I don't know that they're any more lost than you or I."

He leaned in and touched her arm. "I doubt we have *those* kinds of problems," he said.

Right then she spotted me.

She walked over and stood in front of me. "David, what are you doing here?" she said. She put her coat down on a bench, delicately. She reached out to touch my hand, but I stepped back.

I couldn't look at her because my eyes were welling up. I felt the sudden need to be held. I was convinced that if I ran I would find salvation in the snow-covered streets. Amanda's face was very familiar to me, the face of someone I'd wronged before.

I was sure she knew every one of my sins by name.

★ ★ ★

I stumbled into a bar a few blocks away. It reeked of home. The people, sitting there in the dark, all seemed so happy to see me. How I could I refuse them? An overwhelming thirst came over me. I didn't want to abandon sobriety so much as I felt I had to.

When the place closed I slept in the alleyway behind the

bar. I covered myself in garbage bags and shared warmth with the rats. Who, I wonder, can envision the depths of their own despair? I lay there, my body pressed close to the ground, the cold creeping in. I wasn't the only living thing enduring the loneliness of night. But how could I, with my mind lost in the needs of my body, draw comfort from that? And if all the heat finally seeped from me, and then I slipped into a long dark sleep, would any part of me even care? Would my life be any different?

I couldn't stay asleep. I found an all-night diner a few blocks over. It was silent except for the humming of the fluorescent lights. The city was dead, no traffic, no sirens, and I felt, for a few seconds, like I'd walked into a world void of life. I sat at a booth near the door. I made a fuss sitting down, to see if anyone was there. I didn't want to be alone, not anymore.

A moment later a woman appeared. She looked fifty, or maybe a touch younger. Her eyes looked heavy. She smiled. She seemed genuinely happy to see me. As she got closer I was sure I knew her, perhaps because she had the same face as my mother, the same optimistic worry written into the corners of her smile. It didn't matter what I'd done wrong, she was going to take me in, let me rest, even if I was destined to return the same damaged man again and again.

"I have enough for a cup of coffee, but nothing left for tip," I said.

She reached into her apron and grabbed a notepad, took out a pen, and wrote down my order.

"Is that all right?" I said.

"Don't trouble yourself about that," she said. "It's nice to have a visitor."

She turned to walk away but I stopped her.

"I'm sorry about the smell."

She put her hand on my forearm. "I know you're hurtin', honey. I can see that." Then she reached for the cross around her neck, pressed it between her fingers.

"I didn't mean for you to see it," I said.

"Don't worry, sweetie. It'll be all right."

I looked down at my hands, bowing my head so I wouldn't have to look her in the eyes.

"Thank you."

"You sit here just as long as you want," she said.

After that she left me alone, short of bringing refills, to warm up and be with my thoughts, which was a horrible but necessary gift.

Before we went to the VA, Tristan and I had talked about reenlisting. The truth is that part of me missed the war. It was like Tristan said once: 95 percent of the time the war was shit. 95 percent of the time you wanted to get out. But when you left, all you could think about was that other 5 percent when it wasn't shit, when there was something about it that you could never find again.

Our trip to the VA meant that we couldn't return to the Marine Corps. We knew that and we went anyway. I was thankful for it, that that was no longer an option. I didn't want to go back. I finally knew that much.

★ ★ ★

Once the sun came up I put my money on the table and left. I walked a few blocks over and sat on the steps of the municipal building watching people walk to work. I thought about

Doc Johnson. I thought about Tristan and the rest of those guys and what they might talk about that day in group. I thought about going back and trying to give an honest answer.

I looked out over the street. There were men in business suits, women in skirts. They moved with a kind of determination. They had things to do that they truly believed were important. Nothing could shake their confidence, their belief in the promise of better things. All of them seemed to have a bright future.

I wanted everything they had.

SLAUGHTER

Name: Scott ████
Service: Marine Corps
Tour Dates: ████████
Location: Warrior, AL
Duration: 15:13.81

We'd been in Iraq for three days, just over the border from Kuwait, waiting to be assigned our permanent post. Up to this point the war had been mostly boring. My buddy, Nick Bodyk, Bodi, and I had been awake since we'd crossed the border, convinced that if we fell asleep the war would start without us. Then our commanding officer came to our barracks, picked a group of us at random, told us we'd be bagging up civilian corpses, people who'd been slaughtered by insurgents just outside our post. Bodi and I were two of the lucky ones.

Bodi stood on the edge of the pile staring into it, lifted his head to the sky, and inhaled deeply.

"What're you doing?" I said.

"Shit. They smell kind of funny," he said.

"They're rotting," I said. I could feel the stench of it, seeping into my uniform, my pores.

"Yeah," he said. "But it's a real familiar smell, something I've smelled before."

"Spoiled meat," I said. "It's just like spoiled meat."

"No. Rotting pumpkins. That's what it is. Like Halloween, or after Halloween. Rotting pumpkins." He knelt down and reached his hand toward one of the bodies.

"I'd put some gloves on," I said.

Bodi started running his fingers over what looked to be a raw and particularly bloody hunk of flesh. He stopped and held his hand over something that resembled bone. He stood up and wiped his hands on his pants, made this face like he was piecing something together.

"I think that lady lost her head." Bodi knelt down and took another look. "Yeah, I'm pretty sure she's headless."

★ ★ ★

I was standing by the seven ton, the vehicle we were loading the bodies into, with this kid, Elliott, who nobody liked. He was always getting into other people's business, carrying on like he was some kind of warrior sent to better us all, the people of Iraq and his fellow marines.

"Where's Bodyk?" Elliott asked.

"Looking for a head."

"Why doesn't he just piss in the dirt?"

"Not that kind of head, a human one."

"What? Why?"

"Said it ain't right, being without your head."

"Bullshit."

"Serious," I said. "That's what he told me."

I walked over to where Bodi was standing. He was bagging up the headless lady. She was one of the last corpses. Soon, we'd get into Humvees and escort the seven ton to a nearby hospital where the bodies would be cremated or turned over to the families. We didn't know what would happen to them.

Bodi said, "I've looked everywhere, man, but I can't find it."

"Bodi, you're delirious, brother," I said. "You need some sleep."

"How does something like that go missing," he said, as he bent over to zip up her body bag.

"Don't think about it," I told him.

We stood there for a minute holding the bag. I looked at him. "We're Oscar Mike in a few minutes," I said.

We carried the body to the seven ton and tossed it in. Bodi started walking away.

"Come on," he said, "help me look one last time?"

★ ★ ★

After a little while Bodi came walking down the road with a man over his shoulder.

"Where'd he come from?" Elliott said.

"I found him over in a ditch," Bodi said. "Just down the road."

"Al-Qaeda," the man kept repeating. His stomach had a gaping hole in it, maybe the size of a baseball. I was pretty sure I could see his intestines wiggling around inside him.

"Did you do that to him?" Elliott said.

"No. I found him like this," Bodi said. "I'm trying to save his life."

Our field medic, Camacho, walked over then. "Jesus, this guy needs real help."

"That's what I've been saying all along," Bodi said.

He stood there, looking down on the man.

"When did this happen?" Camacho said.

"I don't think he understands English," Bodi said.

"Sir," Camacho said. "Do you understand me?"

"I'll go get the fucking translator," Elliott said, and jogged off.

"Hold this over his wound," Camacho said, handing some gauze to me.

"What's that gonna do?" Bodi asked.

"Well, obviously he needs more than that," Camacho said.

Bodi and I stood there waiting for everyone else to get the things they needed to save this man's life. "There was a lady who had her head cut off," Bodi ran his thumb over his throat. "Did you know her?" Bodi said.

"Al-Qaeda," the man repeated.

"She was Al-Qaeda?"

"Bodi," I said.

"I wish I knew how to speak Arabic. I have so many questions."

Camacho came back, and Bodi said, "He doesn't know anything about the woman."

Camacho applied new gauze and popped the guy with a needle full of drugs. "You're going to be just fine," he shouted at the guy.

"Are you sure about that?" I said. "That's a serious wound."

"Doesn't seem to have hit anything important," Camacho said.

Bodi squatted down next to them. "Freaking amazing," he said.

The translator ran up to us then. He was winded from running. "Did you ask him who he is?" he said, looking at us. He pulled a cigarette from his shirt pocket and took his time lighting it. He wasn't interested in any of this.

Camacho looked up at him, "We got you so you could ask him," he said.

"Yeah, right, of course," the translator said. He bent down and exhaled a giant puff of smoke. Then, in plain English, he said, "What's the problem, bub?"

Bodi and Elliott and I stood guard while Camacho and the translator went to work.

Elliott said, "I bet you think you're going to win some medal on this, don't you? I bet you think you're real hot shit. Don't you know that haji is the enemy? Don't you know that you just saved some terrorist who is probably going to come back and kill you tomorrow?"

"Are you talking to me?" Bodi said. He was watching Camacho work.

"Who else would I be talking to, you moron," Elliott said. "This is war. You should have let him die."

I lit a cigarette and kept blowing smoke directly into Elliott's face. He was annoying me.

Bodi was singing the lyrics to a Dylan song, "If you see her say hello, she might be in Tangier. She left here last early spring, is living there I hear."

"Ward," Elliott said, "what's wrong with your friend?"

"No clue," I said. I looked out over the desert, scanning for vehicles coming down the road. "I'm not worried about him, if that's what you're asking."

"Well, you should be. Look at him. He's a liability."

In the meantime, a few of the higher-ups had come out to see what the situation was. The rest of the unit sat near their vehicles, waiting for the convoy to take the bodies to the hospital, for that part of our day to be over. It smelled like rotting flesh and dust. I popped a few NoDoz, which my mother had sent me in a care package.

Camacho was giving his report to the ranking officers, telling them how he thought they should go about handling the situation. Elliott and I knelt on the road, not talking, scanning for trouble. Bodi walked over to the translator, who was standing next to the wounded man, and I saw him ask a question, but couldn't hear it. Bodi handed the translator a pack of cigarettes in exchange for whatever it was he wanted, and then the translator walked over and talked to the wounded man.

Bodi walked back over to Elliott and me after a short bit.

"What was that all about?" Elliott said.

Bodi stood smoking a Parliament. It seemed like a few minutes had passed, but it could only have been a few seconds. "I asked if he knew the lady's name," Bodi said.

★ ★ ★

An order was issued. We would spread out and look for more survivors.

"I'm pretty sure you saved that guy's life," I said to Bodi.

"Could be," he said.

The wounded man was being treated on base. Despite

76

having a giant hole in his belly, the man was going to walk away with nothing more than a scar. He was being stitched up right then, would be given fluids and some food and sent on his way in a night or two.

"Never seen anything like that," Camacho said. "It's almost like nothing happened. A goddamn miracle if you ask me."

* * *

At some point, the desert is like the ocean. You go out far enough and you get lost in the center. I'd been awake for seventy-two hours, and now my body was ready to collapse under the heat of the sun. I popped a few more NoDoz, sucked on the white tablets until they became a chalky paste in my mouth. Bodi and I stood for a second starring at the flatness before us.

We sat down on the ground, the dust swirling in small cyclones that stuck to our sweaty skin. I could still smell the rotting flesh on me.

"I really want to find that lady's head," Bodi sighed.

"We should get going."

"It'd be something special if I could do that."

"No one cares," I said. "It won't make any difference now. She's dead."

Bodi poured water on his hands, ran them over his face. "That's not the point," he said.

Maybe he thought this would save us.

Soon after that, Bodi found the head. It was just lying there in the desert. It was one of those things you see but can't make sense of, something from a fable or the Bible, maybe. I half expected it to open its mouth and tell us everything. Bodi held it between his hands, very gently, examining it. For a second I thought, because of the way he looked at it, that he might press his lips to it, try to breathe life into it again. He kept holding on like it was a lover, someone he knew from this life or another, searching its features, it seemed, for a memory that I would never see.

★ ★ ★

We weren't lost, not exactly. We could see a town, but it looked very far off.

Bodi cradled the head. "It's not as heavy as I thought it'd be. Wanna see?"

"No, I'm fine."

"It's nothing to be afraid of."

A wild dog ran toward us.

"I don't know about carrying that thing around," I said. "I've got a bad feeling about it. Maybe you should just leave it here, let the dogs have it."

"Why would I do that?"

"Because."

"We have our orders," he said.

"To bring back survivors, not heads."

The dog reached us. "Hey, buddy," Bodi said.

He handed me the head. "Hold this for me." He bent down and put his hand out toward the dog.

"There you go," he said, "you're not so bad, are you?" The dog licked Bodi's fingers.

Soon, Bodi was in the sand, wrestling with the animal, rolling around in the dirt as if he were in his own backyard. "Maybe, someday, I'll be a veterinarian," he said.

A small group of children had gathered on the edge of the town, stood giggling at Bodi. One of them called out, "Look at the dogs, playing."

"Is he yours?" Bodi called back. "Is this your pet?"

"Pet?" the boy asked, and then the children ran away, back into the city.

Bodi stood up and dusted himself off. He pulled a rope from his pack, tied it around the dog's neck, a makeshift leash. He started walking toward the city, a goofy grin on his face. "Let's go return him," he said.

"Bodi," I said, "we need to go back."

"We will." He kept walking. "Just this one thing."

I cradled the head under my arm and followed. Suddenly I felt very attached to it.

"This is crazy," I said.

"It won't take long. One more good deed before the war starts."

As we approached the city, a sandstorm began to rise behind us. Already the sun was being overtaken and our giant shadows were being swallowed, and the sky was turning red. Soon the air would turn orange and we wouldn't be able to see more than a foot in front of us.

Bodi bent down and untied the dog, rubbing it behind the ears before letting it run off.

"I thought you wanted to return it?"

"We need to find shelter," he said. "This storm will swallow us."

We ran to the city, tracking the footprints of the children who'd been there just a few minutes before.

Suddenly we were in an olive orchard. The day had been

oppressively warm to that point, but here, on the edge of this field, the air shifted and I could smell rain coming.

"We're lost," I said.

That was the year it snowed in Baghdad and people thought it was a sign of peace.

"Do you trust me?" Bodi asked.

We vanished in the sandstorm, and, for a second, I worried that I'd lost sight of him. I held the head tightly. I reached out with my free hand to find my friend.

The red dust swirled around us and I heard thunder. I didn't know which way to go. Bodi took off into the orchard. After a bit I couldn't see him anymore, and started screaming, "Bodi, I'm losing you, I'm losing you." He must have heard me wrong because he kept saying, "Losing what, losing what?" I followed his voice into the trees.

There was smoke billowing in the distance and a light washing over everything. It looked close. I imagined Bodi was headed for it.

We climbed further and further up a slope, the trees passing by like the heads of sleeping giants. At the top of the hill, there was a clearing, the only road, I figured, that led there. Bodi stopped, waiting for me. From here the light wrapped around the branches in front of us. The smoke seemed to be coming from the orchard itself. Just ahead we broke into another clearing, and in front of us stood the most magnificent farmhouse, covered in light, each window with a candle in it, lit and burning. Smoke rose from the stack and the whole thing, in the midst of the storm, looked full of light and a kind of hope I had never felt before or since. I thought, if only for a second, that I could lie down right there and sleep the most peaceful sleep I'd ever know.

Bodi lifted his arms toward the sky, said, "It's a farmhouse."

"It's something," I said, thinking that we'd stumbled on more than that.

"It's like a goddamn dream," Bodi said, almost whispering.

"Yeah," I said. "That's what I was thinking."

We climbed the fence surrounding the property; it was made of wood, one of those ones with the three rails plugged into the posts. We worked our way to the windows, peering into each as if there might be something inside that we'd never seen before, some kind of secret that we needed to know. Each room was immaculate, the kind of place our mothers wished they had, the kind of place you might walk into and never want to step out of, ever. Though I've tried over and over again, there is no way to accurately describe it; there is no way to make it real again. We went from window to window, hoping, I think, that we might finally find the owners, catch a glimpse of the people who lived this life. But with each empty room I sensed a great disappointment rising up in us, until, finally, we stumbled upon a room, empty, save for a girl, maybe our age or just a bit younger. She stood, frozen there like some kind of beautiful statue.

We pressed our faces to the glass.

"Are you seeing this?" Bodi asked.

The girl, just then, slipped off her nightgown, began dancing around as if the world had been made for her and her alone. Some kind of music, a fierce, violent, and sad thing, swelled around her. "Is this real. Is this really happening?" I asked no one in particular.

We stood there for some time. It may have been hours for all I know.

Finally, I turned to Bodi, "We'd better go."

"Go where?" he said.

"To base, we've gotta get back."

"Do you still have that head?" he asked.

"Yeah, why?"

"Just checking."

"Bodi," I said. "We're going to get caught."

"Maybe if we knocked on the window she'd let us in. We can say we're lost or something."

We stood there, the sound of the wind cutting through the fields, like a pack of wolves calling out in unison, while she moved with a weightless grace.

At some point Bodi said, "I want you to know I have an erection."

"I wish you hadn't told me that."

"I'm just being honest," he said. "This is the most beautiful thing I've ever seen."

"We should go."

"It's amazing, really, isn't it?"

"Bodi."

"Maybe I can stay here."

"We have to leave."

"Why would we leave now?"

And, honestly, I had no answer for that.

"Sooner or later we're going to have to go," I said, quietly.

"Never."

He pressed his face against the glass, cupping his hands around his eyes.

I leaned in next to him. I was sure now that she knew we were there, that she was doing this just for us.

Bodi said, "We'll never see anything like this again. Not in this lifetime."

"You might be right."

"I know I'm right."

"I understand that."

"Don't you see," he said, "how untouchable it all is?"

"I think I do," I said. "I'm pretty sure I do."

★ ★ ★

I don't know, now, how much of it was real. I know we found the head, and that seemed like a good thing, a sign of hope. I remember that, feeling hopeful about having done something right, even though I'd thought it was a waste at first. The storm was real, too, the air thick and alien, and I remember feeling buried in it, just one more thing trapped here on earth. I knew how a man could claim to hear the voice of God, how He might tell him, yes, he would have to take the lives of other men.

As we walked down the road, headed back to our post, I wanted to ask Bodi something but I didn't know what. I looked over my shoulder. Nothing of the happiness we'd seen or the ugliness we were headed back to was visible. We walked on in silence, the orchard fading more and more with every step we took.

★ ★ ★

We returned just as the convoy was preparing to leave, and it didn't seem like anyone had even noticed we were gone.

"What are you doing with that?" Elliott said, pointing at the head in Bodi's hands.

"She'll keep us safe," Bodi said, "watch over us."

We slid into our Humvee with Elliott and Camacho up front, and me and Bodi in the back. Camacho drove while Elliott kept his weapon pointed out the window.

Elliott turned so he could see Bodi, who was sitting behind Camacho, and talked the whole time.

"Where did you faggots run off too?" he said. "Sodomizing one another in the desert?"

"You wouldn't believe what we saw," Bodi said.

"Unless you killed someone," Elliott said, turning to adjust his sight, "I'm not interested."

Bodi looked out the window. "Nobody died," he said, "not yet."

Elliott nodded at the head. "You should toss that thing, now."

"No," Bodi said.

"It's bad fucking luck."

"Maybe she's an angel now, watching over us," Bodi said. He wasn't joking. He was being sincere.

Elliott turned and looked at Bodi again, gave a loud, fake laugh. "It don't mean shit," he said, "It don't change anything."

Bodi looked out the window, pulling the head closer to him. "Maybe," he said, "maybe not."

★ ★ ★

We were coming up on the hospital when the evening prayer began. There were hundreds of people outside, kneeling before the walls, saying a single prayer in unison. It was the most humbling display of faith I'd ever witnessed.

"Look at these barbarians," Elliott said.

"Barbarians?" Bodi asked.

"Don't let them fool you," Elliott said. "They don't worship the same God as us."

"So what?" Bodi said.

"The God you worship makes all the difference."

"How's that?" I asked.

"Because they kill in the name of that God," Elliott said. "We're here because of this fake-ass religion. You know that, don't you?"

"This is news to me," I said. I scanned my sector for any threats.

"Don't be ignorant," Elliott said.

"Well, how do we stop this?" Bodi said, gesturing to the crowd.

"Are you serious?"

We'd come to a halt a hundred yards before the edge of the crowd.

"The same way we did it with the Indians," Elliott said. "We kill enough of them and they disappear. It's a simple math equation."

Outside, the people spoke to God, and, though I didn't know the language, I understood the meaning.

"I could mow this whole herd down, right now," Elliott said.

Camacho looked at him, "You won't."

"I'm a goddamn Devil Dog," Elliott said.

Camacho said, "I'm not sure what that even means."

Elliott leveled his weapon. "Pop," he said, "Pop, pop." He kept moving his shoulder back as if it were taking recoil.

"Cute," Camacho said.

A voice on the radio spoke, "Everyone, hold your fire."

"Pussy, leftist bullshit," Elliott said, as he reached back and snagged the head from Bodi's hands.

"Give me that."

"What the fuck?" I said, reaching for Elliott, but he leaned forward and I could only get at his shirt.

"I wonder if she gave good head?" he laughed.

"Jesus," Camacho said.

"Give it to me, now," Bodi said, jabbing at Elliott with the butt of his rifle.

Elliott held the head out the window. "Easy does it," he said.

I let go of him.

"That's not funny," Bodi said.

The prayer was ending.

"Oscar Mike," the radio squawked, and we started moving forward again.

Bodi looked at me, he was in a panic.

"Come on, Elliott," I said, "stop fucking around."

Elliott looked over his shoulder at Bodi and smiled, a nasty, full-toothed thing that made him look crazed.

I knew we'd done something important, finding that head. I knew it might be the only decent thing we'd do while we were there.

Elliott was swinging it by the hair now, in big, slow circles.

"Elliott," I said, "quit playing."

"Civilized," he said, as he picked up speed, started making wider passes, so it looked like he might scrape it against the ground.

86

Bodi screamed out, "You're going to ruin it."

The worshippers stood, staring.

"Elliott," I said. I reached for him, but as we moved through the crowd he leaned further out the window, lobbed the head into the air, where it froze, suspended against the sky.

The people looked on without horror. I was sure I saw something like sadness, a kind of sad resignation that this is how things had been and always would be.

I heard Bodi yell, "No." He went for his weapon, or at least I thought he did. But, then he looked at me and said, "We're doomed now. We're doomed."

I watched as the people backed away, as the head fell to the ground, thinking that Bodi was right, that this was a sign of things to come. But how could we know what would happen next? Who could predict such a thing?

We reached the gate. The people stood, frozen for one silent moment, watching as we rolled past. Elliott leaned out the window.

"This is war, motherfuckers," he screamed. "God will not save you."

BATTLE BUDDY

Name: Stephen ███████
Service: Marine Corps
Tour Dates: ████████████████
Location: Erie, PA
Duration: 11:30.62

arrived at the Erie International Airport at 5 p.m. I had just returned home from the war. There was no sign of snow. It was late October, and the leaves were turning. My friend, Josh, was picking me up. He was late so I sat in the airport bar cutting into the $20,000 I'd saved over my four years of service, getting a start on my time home, moving in the direction I'd travel for the better part of that year. But this was the beginning and I didn't know that yet.

After a few drinks I went outside to smoke and wait for Josh. When he arrived he rolled up in a brand new Ford F150. His second tour in Iraq had ended a year ago and now he was working at a home for the mentally and physically disabled, making $2,400 a month and living in his mother's basement.

"What do you think?" he asked as I climbed into the cab.

"Of what?" I said.

"Of my truck? Jesus."

I lit a Parliament, looked around the cab. He had already taken out the factory stereo and installed a custom CD player. The guy in the car behind us leaned on his horn. We sat ignoring it. He honked again and Josh turned the music up.

"Not bad."

"Not bad?" he said, smiling, inhaling his Marlboro and letting the smoke roll out in a giant fog.

I wanted to ask him about his sister, Lora, because I had had a thing for her in high school, had even kissed her before I left for basic. I wanted to know what she'd been doing, if she was single.

The guy behind us kept leaning on his horn. Josh waved him forward and the man pulled alongside us, rolled down his window, and yelled something I couldn't hear over the music.

"This fucking guy," Josh said.

He turned toward the car, flicked his cigarette through the open window.

"Fuck off," he said.

Then he gunned the engine, slid out in front of the guy, pointed us toward the nearest bar, punched me in the arm as we rounded the corner and merged into traffic.

"Welcome home, fucker."

★ ★ ★

All my old buddies had come out to see me. It was a Thursday night and most of them had to work in the morning, some at General Electric, others at Alliance Plastics, and the less fortunate ones at Smith's, the meat-packing plant. For the most part it was good, everyone was happy to see me. "Welcome back," "Made it in one whole piece," "Lucky fucking bastard," that kind of shit. No one wanted to talk about the war yet. Right now they just wanted to let me know I was missed, let me settle back into the routine of it.

But the crowd made me uneasy. The sounds and heat of people overwhelmed me. And Lora, Josh's sister, was there with her new boyfriend, George, and everything else felt irrelevant. I just wanted to put my arms around her, get her alone so I could tell her how much I'd been thinking about her.

"So this is the marine I've been hearing about," George said. He reached to shake my hand.

I hated him instantly.

"Hey," I said. "It's nice to meet you."

George was the type of guy who made loud jokes, had opinions about everything. I was sitting on a barstool moping, watching Penn State take a beating, listening to his analysis of the game. Every part of me tingled as if all my limbs had fallen asleep. My friends were getting me drunk, clapping me on the back. Josh sat down next to me, said, "Don't let him bother you. No one likes him."

I looked over at Lora, who was standing next to George. She was smiling and listening closely like every word he said was full of meaning. I sipped at my beer while old men screamed at the television.

Josh elbowed me, smiled. "You keep staring like that and George is going to think something's up."

★ ★ ★

After a few hours the guys left and it was just me and Josh and Lora and George. Lora was the only sober one. By then I may have been looking to pick a fight. Because, I was thinking, George had come in and taken the woman I wanted while I was away fighting a war. He had shown up to my homecoming and talked the whole time. I felt, now, like he owed me something.

"Steve, what do you think about the war?" George said.

"Honey," Lora said. "Now's not the time."

It wasn't, but I was ready to have it out with him.

The bar had grown quiet and Josh sat next to me, refilling both our glasses.

"Yeah, Steve," he said. "Tell George about the war."

I knew by the way Josh said it that they'd had this discussion before, could tell he was happy to have another marine there to take George down a peg. I thought a good fistfight might make me feel better. There was George and then the jukebox and then pieces of conversation. It all moved in and out, bits of sound, like trying to find the right station on the radio.

"What do you want to know?" I said, looking past George at Lora.

"Is it right or is it wrong?" he said.

"A matter of perspective," I said.

"Perspective?" he said. "Isn't it really a matter of justice?"

"Justice, how?" I said.

Josh had his hand on my shoulder, like he was coaching me through it. "Semper fi," he whispered.

Lora put her hand on George's arm. Maybe she thought that Josh and I were about to gang up on him. Or maybe she knew that Josh and I would only humor him to a point, that the next thing he said could set us off.

"Justice as in, how can you justify the murder of so many innocent people?"

"Murder?" I said. "Are you referring to collateral damage?"

Josh had already told me what to expect. People back home were no longer interested in the war. We weren't going to have the parades the World War II guys had had, but we weren't going to see the protests, be called baby killers, like the Vietnam guys either. Generally, people didn't care. I suppose, because of that, I wanted George to get angry.

"Collateral damage?" he said. "This is human life we're talking about." He was standing now, almost looking down on me as I sat finishing off the last of my beer. Lora looked at me. Josh giggled.

"Georgie," I said. "Calm down."

"It's George," he said and then held his beer in his hand before setting it down again without drinking any.

I had read books, *On Killing, The Art of War,* anything that might make sense of what I was seeing in Iraq, of what I was doing there. Everything I read confirmed what I knew and what George was trying to say. The whole thing had been a waste. We all knew this, marines and citizens alike. But that didn't mean I had to admit it, not to him.

"You're getting angry, George. You're letting your emotions control you," I said. I was feeling lightheaded.

"Murder," George said. "It's murder if you ask me."

The room was spinning a bit but I kept looking at Lora, trying to figure out which side she was on.

"And for what?" George asked. "Nothing has changed, no one is better for it."

Maybe he was right, maybe nothing had changed, but I didn't want to talk about that.

"Are you trying to call me a murderer, George?"

George stared at me for a second. He didn't want to answer the question, I could see that. Josh finished off his beer and stood up, coming around to stand beside me.

George looked back at Lora and then turned to face me again. He opened his mouth to say something but Josh stepped forward and grabbed him before he could, took him by the collar and spun him to the floor. He twisted George's arm behind his back, pressed his knee into his spine.

"What the fuck are you thinking?" Josh said.

Lora stood up.

Josh pressed his knee in harder, gritting his teeth.

I thought, briefly, about letting Josh do whatever he wanted. But people were watching us. "Palmer," I said. "Let him go."

Josh looked at me, smiled. Then he leaned in, put his lips to George's ear.

"This conversation," he said, "is over."

★ ★ ★

After that, they left. Josh and I went outside for a smoke and he showed me restraining techniques, the things we'd been trained to do during basic, the type of move he'd just used on George.

"A guy grabs you like this," he said, putting my hands on him. "And then you do this," he said, guiding me to the ground. "Never let 'em catch you off guard."

Josh told me he used these techniques every day at his new job, when he was trying to calm a patient down. It was funny thinking of him tackling one of those people, most of them so zonked out they didn't know that they had done something wrong. The next thing they know a six-foot-five-inch giant has them pinned to the floor, telling them over and over with that cigarette-scarred voice, "Calm down, calm down."

I could taste the fumes rolling out of Josh's mouth as he pressed me to the ground, as he spun me around and gained control of my arms and hands. It reminded me of watching that show *Cops* and it made me laugh. Josh thought I was laughing at him and tightened his grip.

"What's so funny?" he said, twisting the muscles in my arm so hard I thought they'd start oozing blood.

I could not stop laughing.

★ ★ ★

At some point we stood side by side, the first flakes falling, puking beautiful streams of liquid onto the fresh snow. After ten or fifteen minutes Josh turned to me.

"Don't worry about that fucking guy," he said, wiping his hand across his mouth.

I rose up, ran some snow over my forehead, put it in my mouth, and spit it out. It was coming down fast now and it wouldn't be long before everything was buried.

"Yeah," I said. "No worries."

Already any sign of our sickness had been erased.

It was late, close to last call, but I could see in Josh's eyes that he wasn't ready to go home. "I have something to tell you," he said.

"Okay," I said. We stood six feet apart in the manner of men preparing to draw, wobbling a bit as the wind picked up.

"Let's get another drink, before we head out," he said.

But we stayed there for a few minutes, snow getting stuck in our hair and melting into our faces.

"I hate to be the one to tell you," Josh said, "but this is it. This is what it's like to be home."

★ ★ ★

Josh was driving. I remember falling asleep. Snow was coming down like great clouds of dust from imploding buildings, and then there was a sound that shook me from my dream just long enough for me to realize that I was alive. I was thrust into the passenger side airbag, my head slamming back and forth. My eyes began to water and a warm pool of blood trickled from my nose. When everything settled I sat there, bloodied, but otherwise unaffected. I looked to my left. The driver's side was smashed in, pinning Josh against his seat. In its place the hulking trunk of a willow tree; the tendrils draped around us as if it were trying to swallow us whole. Beyond that, it was dark and the cab was filling with snow. There was the sound of fluid spilling to the ground. As my eyes adjusted I saw that Josh had been pressed flat. His right hand and arm lay limp between us. He didn't make any noise.

Before my dream I remember Josh saying "Don't fall asleep, Stevie. Don't fall asleep." He had both hands tight around the wheel, his face pressed toward the window. He kept blinking and opening his eyes wide and blinking again. It looked like we had driven into the static of a TV screen. The sound of the snow crunching underneath us, the heat from the vents, all of it worked on me something like sleeping pills. I had no idea how long I was out, no idea how close we were to home. I only knew that we were in a field somewhere along Route 20 headed to or from someplace I'll never know.

I told the police that much when they came to see me. They sat with me as I went in and out of consciousness. I was at Saint Vincent Hospital. No one had said anything about my friend or about my condition. I lay in bed, my body hooked up to machines, a monitor beeping over and over again. I wasn't sure which parts I'd dreamed and which parts I'd lived.

"Your buddy's dead," the uniformed cop said after a while.

"Been dead for some time now," said the one wearing a blazer.

I could see, through the cracked door, that there were people waiting in the hallway, but I couldn't tell who.

"Son, are you listening?" the uniformed officer asked.

"Yeah," I said. But I wasn't sure how they wanted me to respond. The light coming from the hallway reminded me of Sunday mass at Saint Margaret Mary, where my father took me as a child. I felt a sudden and overwhelming urge to confess.

★ ★ ★

At Josh's funeral Lora didn't say a word to me even though I stood next to her. Instead, George talked the whole time.

"Jesus, kid lived through a war only to die like this."

I tried to ignore him, tried to focus on the funeral and the marines who stood in their blues holding Josh's coffin, but George wouldn't shut up.

"So this is what you get for joining the United States Marine Corps," he said.

I stared at him, thinking about how I would have liked to beat him bloody right there in front of everyone. I wondered what Josh would have done. I thought about that night and him taking George to the ground. I kept balling my hands into fists, opening them and closing them, lost track of time. Then there was the sound of gunshots, three rounds fired into the sky. Lora reached over and held my hand, kept her eyes straight ahead. Every time those marines pulled the trigger, she squeezed harder, dug her nails deeper and deeper into the palm of my hand.

★ ★ ★

Later that night everyone went to a bar and drank and told stories about Josh, his family and his friends and some of the marines who had served with him. I sat alone, drunk. Lora was with a group of friends, girls she worked with. George had gone home at some point. I watched her from across the room. Her lips were a dark red, a red so deep that it made her mouth look like a separate entity. We didn't speak to one another, in fact didn't acknowledge one another, until late, near last call, when she came up and took me by the arm.

"Come with me," she said. "I want to talk."

I didn't know what to do. I wanted to go. I was afraid to go. I didn't say anything.

"It won't be so bad," she said, and then she guided me the four blocks back to her apartment.

When we walked through the door she took off her clothes without saying a word. I leaned into her then, pressed myself against those red lips. I wanted to tell her everything.

After we slept together, a violent and sad kind of collision, something I'd never felt before, we lay in her bed, the cold of winter pressing in on us. Her room was lit by a single candle. I could make out the shape of her in the dim light but could distinguish none of her features.

"You can talk to me," she said, running her hand through my hair. But I wasn't ready for that.

If I were I would have told her about her brother, the way he looked just before he died, how the snow started piling up around him and on him and how I wanted to reach over and brush it off, but couldn't. I would have told her that I was afraid to move or maybe even more afraid to touch him. I wanted her to understand.

Or maybe what I needed to talk about, even more than that, was the war, how being at war was a fine mix between chaos and order. Sometimes it was all order: cleaning, guarding the post, killing time waiting for the next patrol. But then, in the midst of order, there was the war itself, which was chaos, which we couldn't figure out or bring order to. And sometimes, without the chaos, we went mad, and so we found ways to create it, because that was what we'd been trained to expect. The world would always be violent. It would never make sense.

No one, I wanted to tell her, had prepared us for peace.

AWOL

Name: Gordon █████████
Service: Marine Corps
Tour Dates: ███████████
Location: Austin, TX
Duration: 20:08.87

It was a good time, as war goes. Sure, some bad stuff had happened so far. Merman had been wounded, lost a leg, and sent home. Karns was dead. Eric Oddo, shortly after Karns's death, collapsed in the road during a firefight, lay there paralyzed by fear while the rest of the platoon, from the safety of a berm, called him pussy and faggot, coward, and yellowbelly.

But now, six months into our ten-month tour, things were pretty peaceful. There was talk of switching to soft covers during patrols. IED Alley, the access road to our post, was mostly a ghost town these days, a part of the war that felt more like myth than something that had killed or maimed so many men. The few firefights we had felt like a formality, both sides shooting at one another so that everyone remembered why we were there.

It was a foolish time to run away from a war.

But there I was, pulling guard duty with Eric Oddo when he said, "I'm thinking about leaving."

"Leaving?"

"Yeah, you know, walking away from all this." He looked out across the street and into the desert. The Euphrates could be seen in the distance, the dark scales of a snake slithering away from us.

Oddo was a twenty-year-old kid from some backwoods town in Kentucky. His father, he claimed, had made him join the marines after he got a girl pregnant.

I was tired and ready to leave the war myself. But I didn't think this was serious.

"You just got here, Oddo. Don't you want to give war a chance?"

"I got a girl back home," he said. "Like I told you, I got responsibilities."

"She'll be there."

Just then, Ritter, my best friend, showed up singing, "Doo, doo, doo, looking out my backdoor," that Creedence Clearwater Revival song.

He sat down next to Oddo. He was wearing a stupid, childish grin and humming now.

"What're you so happy about?" I asked.

"Some of the guys bought some live chickens at the market today. Tomorrow night we're having a feast," Ritter said. He lit a smoke and offered one to Oddo.

"No, thanks."

"Celebration is for everyone," Ritter said, looking at Oddo. "You're more than welcome to join in."

Oddo stood and scanned the perimeter. Ritter started singing again.

I stood and put my arm around Oddo. I looked back at Ritter and winked.

"Haven't you heard?" I said. "Oddo is leaving the war."

★ ★ ★

The next morning, he was gone. When I went to get him for chow, his bed was empty, stripped of the sheet and pillow. I looked everywhere, but no one had seen him.

Ritter was standing at my bunk when I got back. "Where's Eric?"

"I'm not sure," I said. "Kid was talking about leaving."

Ritter sat down on Oddo's cot. "I didn't know he had leave time coming."

"Not that kind of leave, dumbass."

I leaned in close so no one else could hear me. "AWOL."

"Shit, that takes balls. Good for him."

"Good for him?" I said. "What the fuck is wrong with you?"

"I think about that often," Ritter said.

Just then Lieutenant Snyder walked in. He was an ambitious officer, who'd done multiple tours in Afghanistan, been part of the invasion of Iraq. He had every intention of climbing up the food chain, and that ambition scared me.

"Williams," Lieutenant Snyder said, pointing at Oddo's cot, "where's your charge?"

He meant Oddo, because I had recently been promoted to

fire-team leader, was supposed to know when and where he brushed his teeth, or shit, or went to sleep. In other words, it was my job to know where he was at all times.

"Sir, PFC Oddo." I didn't know what to tell him. "I'm not sure."

Technically I didn't know where Oddo was, so telling the LT that the kid was AWOL seemed like an overreaction. On the other hand, if he was gone, it might do me some good to come out with it now, look like I was getting ahead of the situation.

"If you don't know where he is, Williams, then you need to find him, now."

I looked at Ritter, which was a mistake.

"Do you want to consult your girlfriend about this first?" Lieutenant Snyder said.

"No, sir."

"Well?"

"Sir, the thing is." I paused again, and the LT got in my face. We were standing chest to chest. I could smell the coffee and eggs he'd had for breakfast.

"Williams, I want a goddamn answer, and I want it now."

I took a small step back. "It appears that PFC Oddo is gone, sir."

"Gone."

Ritter let out a laugh, cracked a smile. The LT turned and looked down on him.

"Ritterbeck, is something funny about this?"

Ritter tried to collect himself. He sat up straight, squared his shoulders.

"No, sir. Not really."

Lieutenant Snyder looked from Ritter to me, and back again. I was sure he was trying to decide which one of us to hit first.

"Sir," I said, "I believe PFC Oddo has left the war. I believe he may be AWOL."

The lieutenant stepped into me then, pushed me onto my cot. He knelt down so that he was face to face with me, again. He scanned the room to make sure no one was paying attention.

"You're telling me," he whispered, "that one of my marines has gone missing, the one you're responsible for, and you're standing around here waiting for someone to come along and tell you what to do about it?"

"Shit," Ritter snickered.

"Shit is right, son."

I knew that Oddo had fucked me. Right away I knew that.

Lieutenant Snyder stood and motioned for us to join him.

We got to our feet, Ritter and I, side by side. The LT stuck his head right between ours.

"Gentlemen," he said, "you will find PFC Oddo and have him returned to me by nightfall, or I am going to call in a Spec Ops to hunt down three AWOL marines."

He stepped back and examined us, the muscles in his jaw tightening. "Do you understand?" he said.

"Yes, sir."

He turned then, without offering further instruction, without repeating himself. He walked down the length of the hall and left without looking at us.

"Fuck," I said, as I began gathering my things.

Ritter stood and sniffed the air. "Did you just shit your pants?" he said.

* * *

The smartest place to look was the haji market where, when the war turned soft, we'd started going to buy food. There were vendors selling hot meals, and produce, and livestock. If a man was going AWOL, the market would be the best place to get supplies.

"You think we'll find him there?" Ritter asked.

"I hope so," I said.

Inside the market the air was thick with human heat. People were packed together, lurching from stall to stall, selling or buying various things. We walked up to a vendor, a man who often sold us American cigarettes, bootlegged Hollywood movies, energy drinks.

"Have you seen a marine come through here today?" I asked.

"American cigarette," he said.

"How much?" Ritter asked.

Ritter dropped his pack and began fishing around for money. I shook my head and focused on the vendor again. "Have any marines been here today?"

"Yes," he said. "American cigarette, Marlboro."

Ritter looked up, picking through the loose change he'd found in his bag. "You got Marbs?" he said. "Sweet."

"When?" I said.

The man looked over his shoulder at his wife, who was hidden in the shade of his stall, knitting or counting merchandise,

I couldn't tell which. He asked her a question in Arabic, then walked over to her and asked it again.

"Spot me a few bucks," Ritter said.

"We aren't here for cigarettes," I told him.

The vendor returned. He looked at me and then turned to Ritter. "You buy cigarette, I tell you."

A line was forming behind us. I could hear people talking, their voices rising, angry, I imagined, at the marines who were holding things up.

"How much for the Reds?" Ritter asked.

"Twenty, American, for carton."

Ritter laid his change on the counter. It looked like, if he counted every penny, he might have two or three bucks.

"Goddamn it," I said. "This is extortion."

I opened my pack and pulled out a roll of cash. I'd been saving some for the trip home, so I could get shit-faced during the layover in Germany. I handed the man a twenty. He leaned down and grabbed a carton of Marlboros.

"You got Parliaments?" I said.

"Come on," Ritter said, "I hate those things."

The man ignored me, put the twenty in his pocket, and pushed the carton toward me. "I saw the man. About one hour ago," he said.

Ritter reached for the cigarettes, but I stepped in front of him. I pulled a pack from the box and held it out to Ritter before pulling it away. "Find Oddo," I said. "Then, you can have these."

Ritter shouldered his gear. "That's not cool," he said, "using a man's addiction against him."

We walked down the street, deeper into the market. I put

Ritter's cigarettes in my pocket and the carton in my pack.

"Ideas?" I said.

"You could have said thank you," he said.

I picked up the pace. "For what?"

"Dude gave us a deal on them smokes."

I stopped, removed my Kevlar, and wiped my forehead with my sleeve. Ritter was getting on my nerves. The heat was making me tired. I felt sick thinking about how far Oddo might have gone in an hour, assuming the vendor was telling the truth.

"Are you gonna help me find this guy, or what?"

Ritter stood at attention and shot me a salute. "Sir, yes, sir."

I looked over my shoulder at the stalls ahead, scanning them for Oddo. I turned back toward Ritter and shook my head.

"Jesus," he said, "there's a town on the other side of the market."

I looked at him.

"You used to be cool," Ritter said, as he walked past me toward the town. He looked like a man who was pleasantly strolling through a park. "War has changed you, my friend. War has gone and fucked you up."

★ ★ ★

We walked a few klicks north, not talking. It felt like a long walk, like this town was a figment of Ritter's imagination.

And then, there Oddo was, playing soccer in a field with a group of children.

"Shit, yeah," Ritter said. "Give me my smokes."

I tossed a pack at him and it bounced off his chest. He bent to pick it up and strolled to the edge of the field. Oddo weaved in and out, passing the ball off to a little boy.

"Dude's got skills," Ritter said.

I stood beside him. "He's playing with nine-year-olds," I said.

"Don't hate."

It looked like the whole village was there, sitting on the sideline nearest their homes, watching the American marine, the runaway, who had joined them for a short bit before continuing on. Men and women, girls, the elderly, everyone had come out to see this strange specimen.

We were on the opposite side of the field. We stood with our weapons at rest, two warriors who'd stumbled into civilization.

Ritter called out, "Eric, Eric, he's our man!" He removed his rifle, his pack, and sat propped against them, his legs stretched out in front of him. He waved at the villagers as he lit a cigarette.

"There's some pretty hot hotties in that crowd," Ritter said.

A group of girls waved back at him, giggling into their hands.

I stood there, angry at Ritter for being himself. I don't know what I'd expected, that he'd chase Oddo, tackle him in front of the whole village, carry him, kicking and screaming, back to base. I knew I was going to have to be the one to do something.

I kicked Ritter, lightly, on his side, "You know we have to take him back, right?" I said.

"I suppose so," he said, but he didn't move.

Oddo, for his part, had not acknowledged us, and instead had moved to the far sideline.

"Oddo," I called out, but he kept running around, passing the ball to the little boys, who seemed more interested in him than they were in scoring goals.

"Oddo."

"Guy's got a way with kids," Ritter said. "I'm sure he'll make a good father."

This reminded me of why Oddo was running, and got me thinking. A man who was leaving to return to his family wouldn't stop in a field to play soccer with children. He wouldn't waste any time, wouldn't risk getting caught.

"Maybe someday," I said. "But I doubt it'll be anytime soon." I sat next to Ritter and lit a cigarette.

The game continued, becoming more organized, more competitive. Oddo never looked over at us, but he also made no attempt to flee. His weapon, his pack, they weren't visible. Maybe he'd taken up with the townspeople. Maybe they'd taken him in, were willing to let him stay for a few nights, before he continued on. Or maybe he was going to become one of them.

★ ★ ★

Eventually there was a break in play. The young boys lay on the ground while their mothers poured water over their heads. A woman around our age offered Oddo a glass of water and he took it.

"See," Ritter said. "The ladies love a man who plays with kids."

"That sounded wrong," I said.

"You're a sick, sick man," Ritter said.

AWOL

The sun was high above us now. We could only sit there for a short time, pretend this wasn't going to end for so much longer.

"Oddo," I called out, standing and raising my hand.

He strolled toward us then with a sad smile on his face. The sort of smile someone has when they know they've been caught but still believe in escape.

"You here to take me back?" he said.

"Not me," Ritter said. "I support your right to choose."

Oddo looked back at the village.

"We have to take you back," I said. "You know we do."

In my mind I imagined him lying to me about his made-up wife and kid, or I imagined him throwing the water in our faces and running, forcing me to chase after him. I could see it, him tearing off and me following, while Ritter laughed and cheered him on. But it wasn't like that.

"I'd rather stay," Oddo said.

"I thought you were heading home," I said.

"I was," he said. But he didn't turn to face me.

"Oddo?"

One of the boys approached us then. Ritter stood and smoothed out his shirt, combed his hair with his fingers.

"I think they like you," Ritter said.

The boy stopped next to Oddo but looked at me. "Would you like to join us for food?" he said.

"You speak English?" Ritter said.

"Yes," he said. "We learn at school."

I bent down and picked up my pack. "We can't," I said. "We have to get back to camp."

"Come on," Ritter said, "we've got time."

We stood there, staring at one another.

"Come, soldiers," the boy said, grabbing Oddo by the hand and tugging him, playfully.

Oddo looked at me as if he were asking permission, but the boy had already started walking so Oddo turned and followed.

"Marines," I said.

Ritter picked up his pack and started following Oddo and the boy. "What?" he said.

I stood there baffled. By the time I thought to say anything they were far enough away so that I had to yell.

"We're marines, not soldiers," I said. "At least we're supposed to be."

★ ★ ★

Inside the air was cool and the room was full of noise and laughter. The children were seated, waiting for the food to be served.

"Please," the boy said, "come sit. Leave things here." He pointed to a spot near the door, where there was already a pile of shoes.

I stepped forward, but the boy stepped in front of me. "No weapons," he said.

Oddo and Ritter were taking off their boots. They stopped.

"Don't be rude," Ritter said.

It seemed very obvious to me that we were putting ourselves in danger, but neither Ritter nor Oddo seemed to understand that. To them we were just visiting friends, there was no war, and there was no other context with which to consider the situation.

"You're joking," I said.

The room had grown quiet. Everyone was looking at us now.

"No weapons," the boy repeated, and he reached for my rifle.

"Easy, kid," I said, blocking his reach with my forearm. "Easy."

Some of the men got to their feet. Perhaps they thought they were going to have to come to the boy's defense. Perhaps they believed I would harm him. But I kept my weapon pointed at the floor so that it was clear I meant no harm.

"Soldier," the boy said, "are you going to hurt me?"

I didn't look at him but instead remained focused on the men, who stood, waiting. They didn't move, but stared at me, watching to see what I would do.

"This is awkward," Ritter said.

I looked around the room. I couldn't tell who my enemy was. They seemed foreign and suspicious. I put my finger on the safety, tightened my grip. I decided that if something were to happen, I would have to shoot the boy first. In all likelihood, he was the bait for any trap.

I counted the number of men in the room, including the boy, and determined that I could take them all with three short bursts. That was a worst-case scenario.

"Oddo," I said, "Ritter. We need to talk, outside."

Ritter turned to step out, but left his pack and weapon.

"Get your things," I said.

Oddo hesitated.

The boy kept looking at us, wondering, I suppose, what he'd done.

No one spoke. I took this to mean that they felt slighted, confused, because they'd done nothing wrong. But they must have anticipated something like this and so felt no need to protest.

I didn't care if they were offended, hurt. I didn't care if they were kind people. I couldn't take a risk on any of that.

I kept my eyes on the room and took one step back. Ritter was standing in the doorway, but Oddo hadn't moved.

"Let's go," I said, "now."

★ ★ ★

Oddo hung his head, waiting for someone to tell him it was all right for him to stay.

"Next time," I said, "don't tell anyone you're leaving."

Oddo looked up at me. "Next time?" he said. "They're gonna put me in prison for this. I'm pretty sure this is it for me."

"The LT will probably make you hand-wash his underwear for a few weeks," Ritter said.

"Something like that," I said.

A young woman watched us from the door. Oddo kept looking back at her. Maybe he thought he could start a family with her. I tried to imagine what that would look like, how long Oddo would survive. Certainly, someone would take issue with him staying. If not someone from the village, an outsider, someone looking to make a point.

"Get your shit," I said.

Oddo turned and walked toward the woman. She had his pack and his weapon. She handed them to him. There wasn't much to say, though I'm sure he wanted to say something.

She looked past him, at Ritter and me, not with hate but with sympathy, like she was thinking how stupid men were, how foolish and childish the whole of our existence was, because of pride, because of fear and honor and duty. Maybe, she thought, if we could only understand this then we could understand Oddo. But I did understand, and I didn't blame him for running. I didn't blame the men who couldn't find it in themselves to be at war.

No one said anything for a while so I said, "Thank you for your kindness."

"If you're ever in the States," Ritter said, "look me up." He adjusted his weapon and started walking back toward camp. He wasn't happy with the state of things, but he was going to do me the favor of leaving it alone.

I stood waiting for Oddo, waiting to see if the woman would make this more difficult for him.

She walked inside, without saying anything, and Oddo stood looking at the empty space where she'd been, imagining, I suppose, that this was the most important decision he would ever face.

I wasn't going to let him decide on his own.

"Eric," I said, before he could make up his mind, "come on, we're going home."

★ ★ ★

On the way back, Oddo confessed that there was no girl back home, no pregnancy. He'd joined the marines because he'd gotten in trouble with the law, was given a choice between serving time and signing up. This, a backdoor draft executed against low-level drug dealers. Some, like Eric Oddo, were not built for war, could not stomach the thought of taking another man's life. And, that, Oddo claimed, was the real issue.

"I don't want to kill anyone," he said.

We'd stopped outside the market so we could get our stories straight, try to make things a little easier on Oddo.

"Maybe, don't tell the LT that," I said, flicking a cigarette into the sand.

"Yeah," Ritter said, "I'd leave that out. Just tell him you got lost in the market, turned around, until we found you."

I stood and then reached down, offering Oddo my hand.

He got to his feet. "Either of you done it," he said, "killed someone?"

"Not me," Ritter said.

Oddo put his pack on, held his weapon slung over one shoulder and off to one side.

Ritter stepped toward Oddo then, adjusted his rifle so that it was in the proper position, angled across his chest and pointed at the ground.

The sun was setting and we needed to get back to base. I started walking.

"What about you?" Oddo asked.

I kept moving, pretending not to hear him.

He caught up to me, walked very close, his hand brushing against mine.

"What about you?" he said.

I stopped and pulled another cigarette from my pack. Oddo stood beside me. He was holding his weapon the wrong way again. If he misfired he'd shoot his own toes off. I lit the cigarette and stood, blowing smoke rings, watching them travel very slowly upward, before they disappeared. I looked at

Oddo and smiled. I offered him a drag, but he declined. All he wanted from me was an answer.

"No," I said, finally, "I can't say I've had the pleasure."

But I had killed a man, just one, early in the war. I wasn't sorry about it, guilty, full of regret. It was a stupid thing Oddo had done, asking a question like that. It was wrong. One marine did not ask another about killing, about death. I could forgive him for not wanting to kill, but I couldn't forgive him for this.

★ ★ ★

Near dusk we returned to base. The sun was melting into the horizon. I could hear the men, inside, preparing their celebration. Whoever was pulling guard duty must have seen us approaching and alerted Lieutenant Snyder, because he was waiting for us at the gate.

Oddo straightened to salute and the LT grabbed him by his collar.

"You have to be the most bootfucked marine I have ever met," Lieutenant Snyder said.

Ritter shook his head, but remained silent.

I looked over at Oddo, thinking about how true it was, how stupid and careless he was. My father told me once, when I was younger, that those who cannot kill will always be subject to those who can. I thought about this as I looked at Oddo. Any thoughts I'd had about how brave a man might be who could walk away from the Marine Corps were gone. Now, I saw him as nothing more than a coward.

"Where have you been all day?" Lieutenant Snyder said, as he released Oddo.

Oddo looked over at me, hoping, I suppose, that I would answer for him.

"Do you want Sergeant Williams to answer for you, son?"

I wish, now, that Oddo had answered for himself. I wish he had had it in him to lie and lie well so that the LT might leave it at that, make Oddo pull extra guard duty or scrub toilets for having been so careless. But he didn't have it in him, not the ability to kill, or soldier, or lie. And so he shook his head, indicated that, yes, despite any better instincts he had, he wanted me to answer for him.

"Well, Williams?"

"Sir," I said, and though I wanted to look over at Ritter, see what he thought of all this, I kept my eyes straight ahead. "Sir, PFC Oddo would like to leave the Corps. He believes, sir, that it was a mistake for him, coming here."

I wasn't trying to get Oddo into any trouble so much as I was trying to make things clear. The kid didn't have it in him. He wasn't a marine, didn't want to be a marine.

"Is that true?" Lieutenant Snyder said, as he took a step toward us.

All Oddo had to do was say yes. He didn't need to explain himself, even if the LT asked. Or he could tell the story about his pregnant wife, about wanting to be with her. But he was too stupid or too honest for that. And, I suppose, he thought confessing would make him feel good, absolved.

"I don't want to be a killer," he said.

The LT looked at me with disgust. I nodded.

"Christ," Lieutenant Snyder said. "This is a new wrinkle." He laughed, and it seemed like a friendly thing, but I knew better. "You're a marine, son. You get paid to kill."

Oddo took a step toward the LT. "You don't understand, sir," he said. He took off his Kevlar and looked into it as if all the answers were hidden there in the bottom.

"I don't want to do it, sir. I won't."

Lieutenant Snyder stepped back, as if Oddo had taken a swing at him. "Won't?"

"I want to go home, sir. I don't belong here."

Oddo tucked his Kevlar under his arm and ran his free hand through his hair. He looked up, for the first time. "I'm not like you," he said.

Ritter and I stood very still. I could hear the men, inside, laughing and shouting. "Catch that fucker," someone said, and then there were the cries of the chickens they'd bought at the market the day before, scrambling to escape their impending slaughter. One of them had gotten loose, was making its way through the front gate, coming toward us.

The LT looked over his shoulder, ignoring Oddo, to see what the commotion was.

The men followed the animal, a mass of hunters approaching us in the dark. They were shirtless and barefoot, some carrying makeshift torches and others with knives and military-issue machetes. "Don't let him get away," they yelled.

The lieutenant turned then, slightly, reached down and grabbed the thing. He held it close to his chest and began cooing. He stroked its head, very softly.

The men came to a halt before they reached us. By now everyone knew that Oddo had run away, knew that something was brewing.

"Gentlemen," Lieutenant Snyder said. "In the future, you will fare better with the creature if you trick it into submission before you try to kill it." He held the bird in his arms without exerting any force to trap it, without worrying that it might run off.

He approached Oddo and held the animal out to him.

"Kill it," the lieutenant said. He removed Oddo's Kevlar and pushed the animal into his hands, holding it there until Oddo took it. The lieutenant stepped back so that he was a part of the crowd now, and because we didn't want to be alone with Oddo, Ritter and I joined them.

Oddo looked down at the feathery thing pressed between his hands. He didn't know what to do with it.

"You have to break the neck clean," Lieutenant Snyder said, "so that it doesn't suffer."

I was sure Oddo was looking right at me.

"Do this, Private Oddo," the LT said, "and all will be forgotten."

I nodded to Oddo. "Do it," I mouthed. My greatest fear, when I'd first come to the war was being like Eric Oddo, being afraid to do the things that must be done. I wanted him to become like me, wanted him to become like us.

"Kill, kill, kill," the men started chanting.

I could see how afraid Oddo was, no matter how dark it'd gotten, that was clear, that part he could not hide.

"Kill, kill, kill," they chanted again, and began moving forward, pressing in on him.

I moved with them.

The LT stood, watching.

Oddo stepped back, but he didn't let go of the bird. Instead, he held it close. He held it tight.

"Kill, kill, kill," we chanted, surrounding him, cutting off any chance for escape.

Days later Eric Oddo ran again only to be caught and dishonorably discharged. But that night we stood together devouring those chickens, half-cooked and poorly plucked, ripped them apart as we fought to get chunks of meat, as grease dripped from our fingers and mouths. There was nothing left. Not a single scrap.

But that is not how I remember that night. Instead, I think about the moment we closed in on Oddo. I found myself next to him, standing so close that I could smell the back of his neck, the sweat, and the fear, and the sadness too. I remember the animal screaming out, trying desperately to get free. The moon froze above us, the broken half of a thing. Me, leaning into Oddo, putting my lips to his ear, whispering, very softly. "Kill," I told him. "Kill."

BULLET CATCHER

Name: Dan ▮▮▮▮▮▮
Service: Marine Corps
Tour Dates: ▮▮▮▮▮▮▮▮▮▮▮
Location: Detroit, MI
Duration: 6:35.93

'd been back from the war for about a week, was staying at my sister's place, sleeping all day and drinking all night, trying to avoid her. She wanted to talk and I wasn't ready for that.

I sat at a bar down the road, drinking half-price beer, because I'd shown the bartender my military ID when she mentioned that her kid brother was in the army. There was a man sitting next to me, maybe a little older, but not by much. He didn't look like everyone else, dress pants, a blue button-down shirt. It was late October, and the leaves were turning that last dark shade before they go dead and flake off. Everyone in the bar stood huddled together, waiting for the first storm to hit, imagining, if the reckoning came, that by some clerical error, lost in the purity of all that fresh snow, they'd be forgotten, be left there to suffer.

The guy next to me kept looking over, taking quick glances as if he were trying to place me, figure out how he knew me. I thought, at first, that he was drunk and confused. Or maybe he was having trouble with his glasses.

Either way, this went on for a while before he said, "So, you were in the service?"

"Yeah," I said.

He bought me a shot of whiskey and told me that he was in the army, had served in Iraq. I made a bit of a joke about it, "Beautiful country over there," which was my way of seeing if he was telling the truth. Because, when you're talking, one veteran to another, you never say, "What a shithole that place was," or "I hate that fucking place." You say, "Beautiful country," "Real vacationland."

He was lying. I knew this because of the way he talked after that. He didn't get the joke. He thought, by spinning me some lines that he could win me over, make me believe. "Those people, I mean, animals. You understand what I'm saying?" he asked. "You've seen it firsthand, right?"

"Sure."

He had a lot of opinions about the people of Iraq, about the war. I envied guys like him. I thought, how nice it must be to have opinions, how wonderful. I wasn't going to tell him anything. I didn't owe him that, but I was willing to listen if it meant more whiskey.

After a while, he invited me to go downtown with him. I don't know why I went, except that maybe I thought it would be better drinking with someone—even if it was this wretched man—than it would be drinking alone. Either way, we hopped in a cab and sped off into the night with the eager look of murderous men drawn across our faces.

The club we arrived at, in the heart of the city, was a hideous, pulsating thing, full of unfortunate hangers-on, men and women who did not know that their best days were behind them. When our drinks arrived, the man raised his glass for a toast. "To the dead," he mumbled before downing his drink and gently placing the glass on the table.

He looked away from me and smiled, a crooked snake-like grin.

"You should have seen this buddy of mine," he said, pausing, pushing his glasses up his nose. "Both of his hands were blown right off. Do you know what I'm talking about? Have you seen anything like that? From the elbow to the tips of his fingers, gone. Just like that. There one second, gone the next. Like some kind of demented magic trick. And the guy, this buddy of mine, he doesn't even notice. He still thinks he's pulling the trigger on his weapon, screaming out 'Die, haji, die,' over and over again."

He turned his empty glass upside down and shook his head, as if this were the most heartbreaking story anyone would ever tell. He looked up at me, trying to see if I had been moved one way or another.

I chuckled. I knew that he wanted something from me. Condolences, maybe. A story of my own. People are sick that way.

"Hey," he said. "You see anything like that?"

I shook my head, tired.

"None of that happened," I said.

"What? What are you talking about?"

"What's your buddy's name? What kind of service weapon was he carrying?"

His face twisted up as if his whiskey had gone down the wrong pipe.

I had no idea what his intentions were. Maybe he was a reservist looking to hear some real war stories. Or maybe he was a reporter. Maybe he wanted to suck my dick. Either way, he wasn't going to admit to any of that.

"You owe me for those drinks," he said.

"Sure," I said, standing so that I could look down on him. After a few seconds of silence, I turned and walked toward the door.

He started screaming to anyone who would listen. "Grab that man," he said. "He's stolen something from me."

No one seemed to notice or care. Men stood, examining one another's shadows.

Down the road there was a VFW hall, where I would later learn to drink in the company of veterans, because the men who'd actually been to war did not need you to talk about it even though that's what we sometimes did.

When I got near the parking lot, I saw a man beating a woman over by the dumpsters. I could hear him hitting her with his fists. It sounded as if someone were chopping wood with the wrong side of an ax.

I hollered, "Hey, buddy." I thought that if he saw someone watching he might have enough shame to stop.

"Fuck off," the guy said, looking up long enough to make eye contact with me before he set his attention on the woman again.

I stood on the opposite side of the parking lot. "You need to stop," I said.

He stood. "Mind your own business."

He had a doughy face, swollen eyes, and a massive scar running down the right side of his head. He wanted to say something else but he seemed dumbfounded by this sudden disruption.

"If you leave her be," I said, "I won't have to get involved. Do you understand?"

"What are you going to do about it," he said. "You don't look like the type."

"I'm a marine," I said, though I'm not sure why.

"That's cute."

"Take it somewhere else," I shouted. But I'd started walking toward the building.

"That's what I thought. Run along now."

When I reached the door, I stopped and said, "I'll call the cops."

"No," he said, "you wouldn't do a thing like that."

During all of this the woman didn't try to escape but instead lay there very patiently waiting for it to end.

"Look, buddy—"

"Listen," he said, "no one expects you to do anything."

I imagined firing an Mk 19 at his face. The explosion, his skull caving in.

The moon was a silver sliver with black splotches. It was one hour until last call.

The VFW parking lot was around back with an alley that divided it from the building across the way. I reached for the door, my hand hovering above the knob, quivering in anticipation. I could only imagine what the inside looked like because the place had no windows facing the lot. Standing there I thought, who will ever know that I walked away?

I looked behind me and saw, towering above me, on the other side of the alley, the back side of an apartment complex. Two women sat on their balcony watching. One of them was shaking her head. I imagined them telling the other residents about the man who let a woman get beat in the back alley, about the veteran who didn't have the courage to save her.

Two women are out smoking cigarettes and gossiping one night when they spot a man hitting a woman in the parking lot below. Neither of them thinks to phone the police. Neither of them calls down. These women, they are embarrassed, they are afraid. Perhaps they are familiar with this kind of violence. What decent person would expect them to do anything other than look away?

I turned the knob, preparing to step inside. Before I did I called out, "You're a coward too," but it wasn't meant for anyone in particular.

As soon as the door closed behind me, I left that other ugliness behind, stood taking stock of the place, the saddest establishment in the whole world. There were only a handful of men, sitting at the bar and mumbling confessions into their drinks. I took a few steps forward. The room was nothing but a cinderblock rectangle with a bar and a jukebox, a bunker where hideous men went to hide. Looking at it, I thought, I have finally come home.

I'd just taken my seat at the confessional when the woman from outside stumbled in. She was bruised up already, her hair a tangled mess. She sat next to me on a barstool.

"I'm sorry about that," I said.

"Not a problem," she said, trying hard to smile.

I looked away from her momentarily. She was monstrous, especially in the dim light. No one else was paying attention to her.

"Let me buy you a beer," I said. The makeup she wore ran down her face. Her eyes were a brilliant shade of blue. "I could do that much, at least."

She touched my hand gently.

"My man's waiting out back," she said. "He's waiting."

"Will he go away soon?"

"Once you go out."

"Me," I said. "What does he want with me?"

"You know."

She ran her fingers through my hair.

"We could escape out the front?" I offered.

She traced the outline of my earlobe. The only thing to do now was go out and take my beating, or run away. I wasn't especially fond of either option, but I knew she was going to try to push me in one direction or the other.

"I'm not going to fight him," I told her.

"If you don't, he's going to take it out on me," she said. "It's you or me this time."

"Did he put you up to this?"

"That doesn't matter now."

She gave me a soft tap on the chin. "You can do this, bullet catcher," she said.

"Don't call me that."

"Come on," she pleaded. She put her hand next to mine on the bar.

"Does this happen often?" I asked.

"Sometimes."

"Sometimes?"

"If you don't, it'll be me."

"You want me to save you, is that what this is?"

"I'm not the one who needs saving."

I stood and took her hand, squeezing it lightly, and then followed her over to the door. I stepped out into the parking lot, raising my hand to shield my eyes against the light. There he was, waiting, just like she'd said. She stood off to one side, kept calling out for one of us to whip the other one's ass, though I'm not sure who she wanted to win. The broken clavicle. The oil-black sky. My fist to his face or his fist to mine.

ON THE EUPHRATES

Name: Michael ███████
Service: Army
Tour Dates: ████████████
Location: Los Angeles, CA
Duration: 7:49.84

Halfway through our tour Hildebrandt, our field medic, was killed on IED Alley. I remember a sharp popping sound. A man who smiled at me as our Humvee passed him by. Ten children, lined up and perfectly spaced out, their hands raised and waving at us.

That morning we woke to James Darbee's screams, his legs kicking at the air in a panicked rage. His cot rocked from side to side so furiously that his pillow fell to the floor. We all circled him. We'd only been asleep for an hour when the screaming started. Someone grabbed a pillow and made like they were going to hold it over Darbee's face.

"Do it," someone whispered.

None of us slept after that, and then, beneath anemic

clouds that wore the sad smiles of circus clowns, we sped toward our mission with great disdain. We babysat army engineers while they filled potholes left by IED explosions, and that day we greeted them with the kind of hatred people usually reserve for their worst enemies. When we stepped from our vehicles, any hope we had of standing on our own feet had melted away. Darbee and I stood back to back, propping one another up, our weapons trained on the stretch of road before us. Darbee went on and on about his dream.

"It was real, I mean, I saw it like that. We were on this road and there was an explosion, and then I was dead. You guys were all standing around laughing because there was shit oozing out of me, puddles of it oozing out my asshole."

My dream was nearly identical, but I didn't tell him that.

"I could smell it," he said. "The shit, it smelled like the Euphrates."

He walked off to find a cigarette after that and I went off to find someone else to lean against.

We left an hour before sunset. Then, a few klicks from base, we gave up on the war, sat back in our seats, stuffing our mouths with haji energy drinks and cigarettes just to stay awake. I stared directly at the setting sun so that I couldn't close my eyes to sleep without seeing volcanic flashes of light.

We lurched down a road that followed the Euphrates. It looked like a fresh wound cut into virgin flesh. We'd been taking that same route for a week by then, driving out at sunrise and returning at sunset so the road could be completed on time for a news story about progress in Iraq's struggle for freedom and decreased violence in the region. We were so sunburned, sleep-deprived, starved that we didn't even raise our weapons to watch our sectors. The engine hummed a frantic song. I'd been eating NoDoz by the fistful so that my eyes were lacquered open. Darbee kept going on about how his number was up, about that dream, about how it was so real he could taste it. As I mentioned, I'd had the same dream, knew, as we approached the tiny village along the banks of the river, that one of us was going to die.

I was too exhausted to care which one of us it was.

When we reached the village, we moved slowly down the road, maneuvering around craters left by recent blasts.

"Wouldn't it have made more sense," Pizzo said, as he guided us toward home, "for them to start at our camp and work toward the FOB?"

"That's it," Darbee said. "It's our own stupidity that's going to kill us."

I sat in the backseat while our convoy wound its way along the Euphrates and into the village. I saw the smiling man, just then, and felt a great dumb grin forming on my face. The moon hovered off in the distance, a bruised piece of fruit waiting to be thrown away. Darbee sat next to me mumbling, "Any second now, any second."

In those days children were used as timers, spaced out so that bombers could count the seconds between each vehicle, could detonate their devices with greater accuracy. When we passed the last child there was a roaring explosion, something you might expect to hear as you watched a giant building brought to its knees. Our vehicle shuttered to a halt and Darbee let out a girlish wail, as if we'd been the ones, as if we'd been flipped over and tossed in a ditch.

We'd both known, or thought we knew, what was going to

happen. But Darbee wasn't ready to admit that it hadn't happened to us.

"Jesus," he said, "fuck."

I ran my fingers over my face. "We're fine," I said, even though I didn't believe it myself.

The children took off running. I leaned out the window and saw that the lead vehicle had been hit. A smell, which I knew was human flesh, spat into the air and snaked its way into my mouth. After a few seconds, I opened my door and stepped out into the street, raising my weapon against imagined enemies. I looked toward the bombed Humvee. Smoke was rising from it. I couldn't see anything else. It was possible that everyone in it was dead. But then there was sound coming from it, men calling out to one another, checking to see if everyone was all right. They sounded peaceful, dazed, and sleepy.

Darbee had yet to realize that he was alive and started to panic, thinking he'd died and was now doomed to spend eternity with us. I turned to see his bloodshot eyes. I thought he'd lost his mind because, when he spoke, his voice was filled with a kind of sickened anger.

"I can't be trapped here with you fuckers," he said.

"James," I said.

Suddenly I cared about being alive, about convincing him of it.

"We're okay," I said, although I couldn't speak for the men ahead of us.

He looked out his window. "We're dead. We've died and this is some kind of sick punishment, isn't it?"

"I'm going to help the others," I said.

He turned to look at me. "No one can help us now."

"You're alive," I said, and playfully slapped him in the face a few times.

Pizzo sat very still in the driver's seat while Tucker reached back and grabbed Darbee's rifle. It seemed like the right thing to do.

"You can have it," Darbee said. "I won't be needing it."

Tucker pulled the weapon from him.

"It's okay," I said, as I turned and ran toward the wounded men.

"You can't save them," I heard him call after me.

I ran, so desperate to see who'd died that I ignored all protocol. It was freezing. I remember my breath pushing out in frozen bursts, my lungs burning. I could see a man, lying next to the lead vehicle, his body charred and giving off smoke. His flesh had turned to slush.

As I approached the passenger side, nearest the dead man, I could hear a faint sucking sound. Hilde sat there, his neck sliced in half, so that his head tilted to the left and the wound looked like a gaping mouth filled with blood. The rest of the vehicle appeared to be fine, no damage to speak of, not even a dent. I stood, staring.

The others, the men in the vehicle, began to rush toward Hilde's side. They pushed me out of the way so that they could move him, try to save his life before he died.

But he was already dead.

I sat on the ground next to the charred corpse. Pizzo and Tucker stood next to me as the others screamed into Hilde's face.

"He's gone," I said.

"What about this guy?" Tucker said.

The dead man had a welding suit strapped around him. I could see that it had contained the blast, though later we'd find out that a buckle had popped off, that that was what had killed Hilde.

"Is he dead?" Tucker asked.

I began laughing uncontrollably. Everyone turned to look at me, because none of them knew what I was laughing about, none of them found this funny. But that only made me laugh harder.

Once I gained control of myself, I asked, "Where's Darbee?"

"Martinez, what's wrong with you?" Pizzo said.

Nothing. I was only relieved that it hadn't been me, but couldn't say that. How could I let them know that I was filled with joy now that I was certain that I was not the one?

When Darbee finally wandered over I took him off to the side and confessed.

"Remember that dream?" I asked him.

"I was sure it was real," he said. "Have you ever had a dream like that?"

"I have," I said. "I have."

As we walked back to meet the others, I could see that the bomber was still alive, taking pathetic little breaths that would surely be his last, because his body was a smoking hunk of stewed meat. There was a sound, like water slowly flowing down a drain. But there was no blood, or at least none that I could see. I knew I was supposed to hate him, was supposed to see him as nothing more than a crazed animal. But I felt sorry for him, thinking he might be alive enough to suffer.

Not sorry because I pitied his circumstance, but because I'd been convinced by my dreams that I would end up just like him.

There was a short-lived debate about searching the village to find out who else was involved, talk of roughing up civilians. Someone even suggested dropping ordnance. A few of the guys were pretty angry.

I was ready to crawl into my cot and dream, so that I might find out which one of us would be next.

After a while, Pizzo said, "Odds are good they're gone anyway."

Shortly after that, we strapped Hilde's body to the hood of a Humvee. There was no interrogation, no retribution, not this time anyway. Instead, we sped off into the night. No one talked during the ride.

Another vehicle dragged the corpse of the bomber behind it. There was nothing left when we arrived back at camp. Our CO said that the body parts, splayed across the road, might show our enemies the cost of bombing us.

"Or make them do it more," I whispered.

"Martinez," the CO said, "do you have something to offer?"

"No, sir."

I had plenty to offer but nothing I intended to say out loud.

Someone draped an American flag over Hilde's body. A few guys carried him. The rest of us stood in silence as they moved past.

"Lucky bastard," Tucker mumbled, once they were gone. "At least he doesn't have to go and do it again tomorrow."

Shortly after they flew Hilde away, each of us met individually with a combat stress counselor.

"How do you feel about what happened today?" he asked me.

Pretty good, I thought, I'm alive.

"Fine," I said.

"Fine," he repeated. "Can you be more specific?"

It struck me that this guy sat in an air-conditioned office all day waiting for moments like this. *What is war really like*, he wanted to know. *How does it make you feel to be a warrior?* He was probably going to study psychology at Harvard when he got home, write a paper about post-traumatic stress.

"It's okay," I said, "stuff like this happens all the time."

He rolled his eyes, sighed.

He decided on a new course of action. "Have you been having dreams?"

I saw myself lying on the side of the road, shit spilling out of me.

"Nothing special," I said.

"Why don't you tell me about them anyway?"

"I'd rather not," I said.

Everyone stood around laughing at me, holding their sides, falling to the ground. There were explosions all around them, but they kept on laughing.

"Have you ever seen the crater an IED makes?" I asked.

"I'd rather hear about your dreams," he said, and reached across the space between us.

Each night it's different. Each night it's the same. At sunrise we wake. The sky stands empty above us. The road goes on for miles. The smiling man. The waving child. Sometimes I'm the one who stands there laughing. Sometimes I'm the one who's died.

ON LEAVE

Name: Kevin ████
Service: Marine Corps
Tour Dates: ████████
Location: Anchorage, AK
Duration: 8:10.60

I walked into the VFW and saw Billy Chapman wearing his Marine Corps blues, his gloved hands wrapped around a pint and his face covered in the kind of joy all warriors feel when they get their first taste of home. The women, girlfriends and wives and daughters of servicemen, circled around him as if he were the only man in the whole VFW hall. It was a sobering, patriotic event. Billy had returned home a hero. The Corps had flown him in straight from Iraq. He'd served his country and now here he was, on leave, the guest of honor at this Fourth of July event. I felt a kind of sick envy, a nausea that could only be explained when one considered the types of dreams I'd had about my own return home, parades and women and a celebration about the fact that I had laid my life on the line to defend the American Dream.

I hadn't known a single person, until now, who had come home to the kind of fanfare Billy was getting, the free booze, the story in the local paper spanning two full pages, with photos of his bright, young, enthusiastic face. This was the culminating event in his heroic return, something akin to pinning a ribbon on the beauty queen. Local politicians and small-time celebrities were there, and I was confused about how a kid, as incompetent as I had remembered him, could go on to do such great things, how he had for so long, during our time in the same neighborhood and at the same school, lived without much notice.

Billy was a runt, younger than me by two years, and I had, when we were younger, as so many people did, poked fun at him, thought of him as the harmless Chapman kid. I was shocked, even a bit jealous, that he'd gone on to become a kind of legend. It seemed to support my theory, that I would make nothing grand of my own life.

There, in the VFW hall, Billy Chapman looked so polished, so put together, that he might well have walked out of an advertisement for the Marine Corps itself. I took stock of the place. It was a square, dark room, like a bunker covered in all kinds of confetti. Everyone there seemed to have forgotten what it was normally like, quiet and lonely, and instead they all laughed and danced and made jokes celebrating Billy and the nation's independence. The walls were plastered with streamers and every surface was covered in some kind of patriotic slogan.

"This is too much," Billy said.

"Tell us your story again," one of the women said.

"There isn't much to tell." He lifted his beer slowly and swallowed half of it as if he were replaying the events that had brought him here, trying to find a new wrinkle, a detail he had yet to tell.

"You're some kind of hero, kid," the mayor said, his hand on Billy's shoulder.

"Bullshit. It ain't like that," Billy said.

He looked up and smiled at me for the first time.

I had never seen the VFW like this. I'd spent a lot of time there, once I'd returned, sitting with the three or four old-timers who went every night. Nothing good ever happened. We all left a bit worse off, it seemed, but I always found my way back.

Every night, as the doors swung open, I imagined I might walk in and find something new, some kind of miracle. We had, most of the younger men who'd enlisted, come home seeking an identity, a direction, and as we shared beers and stories we truly believed we might find one. But by the time we stumbled out, our best stories told and retold, we returned to our beds the same sad, lost bodies, the same boys who had come home without a sense of purpose, without an idea about who we were or where we were headed.

That night, I sat at the bar with a soldier named Mitchell Flowers, who had grown up in the same neighborhood as Billy and I. He had a wonderful afro that puffed out like a kind of halo. When we were kids he was a junior boxing champ. The army had recruited him for just that reason. But then he went into the infantry and suffered a severe concussion that went and ruined his brain and his coordination. His boxing days were over. He'd become a regular at the VFW just like me, which was especially sad, because at one point his whole life stood before him. For the veterans like myself, he had once been a symbol of hope, because I believed I might somehow find my own direction, something like Mitchell once had. Hearing him tell stories about big fights and prize money made it easy to imagine that we could all attain a certain level of celebrity, even if it was only by living through his stories.

"Look at this right here, a celebration," Mitchell said with a tired smile.

Mitchell, who was a kind of local celebrity himself, didn't receive his normal welcome because of it.

He passed me a shot glass full of whiskey and said, "I came down to see this wounded warrior everyone's been talking about."

Then he downed his drink, gesturing for me to join in.

"Wolfe, I'm not going to be around much longer. I wanted to see you one last time," he said, waving his hand at the crowd. "I'm headed down the road to the VA hospital to get my shit straightened out."

Mitchell turned and hugged me like a child seeking comfort. He was wearing his dress blues, too, though his jacket was unbuttoned, his shirt untucked, his combat boots untied.

Then it dawned on me that Billy hadn't come home a hero, or that his story was more complicated than that. One of his cousins, or a friend, or somebody from the neighborhood had mentioned to me that he'd been injured just three weeks into his tour. They didn't, at the time, know the full extent of it, but I recalled something they'd said, "Done for, over and out, finished." Staring down the length of the bar, I finally saw how truly unlucky Billy looked, like a man who was one number off from winning the lotto.

What's worse was, for the first time, I realized that Billy Chapman wasn't home on leave, as if he were going to return to the war again someday, but that he was home for good, that this whole mess was about the fact that, in all likelihood, there were a lot of things Billy would never do again. He'd been paralyzed from the waist down. Out on patrol, during his third week in country, an IED, hidden inside a dead body, detonated behind him. Struck in the back by shrapnel, he had lost all feeling and movement in his legs, and now the doctors were telling him that he could, though they didn't know when or how, maybe, one day walk again. This was what the profile in the paper was about, his struggle to recover, to become whole again. I'd been so focused on my own plight that I hadn't bothered to understand.

This is how it was at the VFW because, to some degree, we all thought we had it worse than the next guy. That's why the marines picked on the army guys and the army guys on the air force and right on down the line. We all believed we were special. Part of it was about ego and tradition and posturing, but another part of it was about self-pity, about feeling like nobody on the face of this earth knew what it meant for you to have seen and done the things you did.

Billy, despite losing three pints of blood, had been brought back to life. The Corps wanted him to tour VA hospitals overseas, because he still believed in the mission, and they believed that his positive outlook might rub off on the guys who were starting to have second thoughts about war and soldiering and giving up their limbs for the nation. He tried it for a time, visited hospitals in Iraq, Afghanistan, Kuwait, but it wore thin, seeing all those injured men, hearing their stories and sometimes their anger, and Billy returned home to serve out the rest of his time at a clinic doing physical therapy and filing paper work.

This was his life at twenty.

Billy was the cornerstone of this Fourth of July event. But in truth, it was all an act, because people had soured on the war, or maybe, more accurately, they'd lost interest. As for me, I'd been working a shit job at a paper mill, the girl I'd been seeing had left me, and now I was left waiting for the day when my miracle would come.

That night, after the celebration wound down, Mitchell Flowers and Billy Chapman and I went out on the town together, searching for trouble or love, we didn't know which.

Billy sat on one side of me and Mitchell on the other. People washed around us in a sea of happiness that we could not understand, but remembered as a part of some phantom life. I considered that and how, I think, all of us wished we could trade places, even with the saddest cases in the joint, just to live one day free from our own skin.

Between us, we had all of fifty dollars. Mitchell and Billy were waiting on disability checks. I had spent most of my money drinking alone at the VFW. We drank every last dime we had.

When the money was gone, we went to Billy's place, where he had a stockpile of drugs, some for anxiety and others for sleep and more still for pain. He hadn't taken any of them, but instead stashed them in a filing cabinet, afraid that if he took them he would let go the drive to walk again, afraid that he might become hooked on them and then lose his mind along with his legs.

In Billy's apartment we sat, an array of pills laid out in front of us.

Billy turned to me. "Wolfe, what's your story, hanging out with two cripples like us?"

"Where else would I be?"

"Out getting laid, college, back at war. Anywhere but here," Billy said.

"I guess I'm a little lost is all."

"Fuck, Wolfe, we're all a little lost," Mitchell said.

I didn't tell them this, but in some ways I envied my friends. After all, no one would ever question the choices they made, the drinking, the pills we were about to swallow by the fistful, because they would assume that their injuries explained their behavior, in some way excused it, and I had no explanation for the things I did.

Then Billy said, "The worst part, you know, about the legs. It isn't that I can't walk. It's that they're still here. I look down at them every fucking morning when I wake up, refusing to do anything I tell them to do."

We shoveled the pills into our mouths, mixed them up and washed them down with the lone beer left in Billy's fridge. I don't remember how Mitchell and I made it to his place, even though it was only a few blocks away. My spine was on fire and my brain felt like a limb that had fallen asleep. Within minutes Mitchell was slumped in a lawn chair. I could hear him mumbling, "I believe, I believe," just like that, over and over again. The last thing I remember thinking was that I wanted to rush to join him, to stumble into his dreams, because it sounded to me like Mitchell was, just then, meeting the Messiah for the first time.

As for Billy, I cannot speak of his dreams. A few days later they found him hanging in his closet by a necktie. They ruled it a suicide, but I knew better than that. Because, for a time, it came to me in flashes, strange dreams that appeared, usually, when I'd been drinking. So I drank more and more. Sometimes we'd be back in the VFW celebrating with Billy. Other times he'd be out with Mitchell and me. But then there were times, and those were the worst, when it was just Billy and me. I could see the panic in his eyes, but I knew that he didn't want me to help him. Outside the sky was bright and blue, the most beautiful day anyone had ever seen. Billy looked at me. He was trying to tell me something. I leaned in close, could feel faint breaths against my cheek.

"Stand up, you worthless piece of shit," he said. "Stand up."

THE CUMULATIVE EFFECT

Name: Tully ███████████
Service: Army
Tour Dates: ████████████
Location: Columbus, OH
Duration: 19:02.46

n April, one month after my father went off to war, leaving my mother and me behind, my mother made me dress in a button-up shirt and one of my father's ties and she took me out on a date. That's what she said: "We're going on a date, mother and son."

I was seventeen. The invasion of Iraq had come and gone and then the hunt for Saddam Hussein began. I imagined my father hunting him, hiding in remote locations or marching for days through the desert. We lived in Columbus, Ohio, in a house on the east side. My mother worked part time as a waitress at a little diner around the corner from our house called The Blue Danube. My father would never have allowed us to eat at a fancy restaurant. In fact, I couldn't remember ever eating out before that night, so I was shocked when we went to a swanky restaurant in the Arena District.

I pressed my mother about that. "How can we afford this meal?" I asked.

"Combat pay," she said between bites of her sixteen-ounce steak. "It's the one good thing your father ever did for us."

"Does Dad know about this?"

My mother set her fork down and wiped her mouth on the cloth napkin. She rubbed her chin like she was thinking about something, and then she picked up her fork again, waving it in front of her while she spoke.

"What he doesn't know won't kill him."

I wasn't comfortable being in a restaurant. Mainly because I had only been in them on our infrequent visits to my mother's parents. I wasn't really sure how to act. But, also, I felt like we were betraying my father's wishes. I picked at the steak my mother insisted I order.

"Do you think he's coming back?" I asked.

My mother put her fork down again, this time making eye contact.

"Honey, we aren't that lucky. He'll be back."

★ ★ ★

My father was a brutal man. At times I hated him, but I was conflicted about his leaving, or more conflicted than my mother seemed to be.

By brutal, I mean that the man was strict. Rigid. He was a military man as was his father and his father's father and so on. I was expected to follow in the long line of Fitzsimmons men who had joined the military and made careers of it. There would be no college for me, save West Point.

A few months before my father went off to war he said, "Tully, I'm just trying to make you a man."

My bed was to be made the same way every morning and I was to report to breakfast, on school days, by 0800 hours. A mislaid sheet, a minute late to eat, an untucked shirt, all of these resulted in boot camp punishments.

"Drop and give me fifty," my father would shout.

"Dad, here?" I looked down at the kitchen floor. "On a school day?"

"Now," he'd say, dressed in full uniform, prepared to head to the recruiting station where he worked.

He also built a mini-obstacle course in our backyard. It was complete with monkey bars, a six-foot scale wall, and eight tires he had laid on the ground side by side in columns that we ran through. On weekends we'd go out at seven in the morning and drill for hours at a time. My father would set up his antique Victrola and play "Semper Paratus" over and over again.

"Do you know what it means?" my father asked.

"What?"

"The title of the march?"

"No," I said.

"It means 'always ready,' Tully, which is what I'm trying to make you."

My father timed me as I ran the course and then I timed him. We compared our results. With each pass he'd add in new wrinkles, smoke grenades or small booby traps, to keep me thinking on my feet. The ultimate goal was for me to surpass my father's times.

For my mother the punishments were different, but they had the same cumulative effect. Meals were to be served at

0800 and 1800 hours, respectively. The house was to be vacuumed and dusted, laundry washed and folded, on a set schedule, one that she could not deviate from. My father punished my mother by withholding things, mostly money, though he would sometimes lock her in the laundry room until she'd done the laundry she'd forgotten, or lock her out of their bedroom until she finished vacuuming and dusting.

"Vacuum at midnight?" my mother said. "Are you crazy?"

"Every soldier must pull their weight," my father said.

★ ★ ★

"Freedom," my father had once told me, "will make a man think he can live his life without discipline, Tully. But it is discipline that ensures his freedom."

I should have seen, the night we went on our date, that my mother was changing. We hadn't talked about my father after she assured me he was coming home. Most of the meal she spent quizzing me about school, the girls I liked, the subjects I was taking. She had always taken a serious interest in me, felt the need to try and offset the discipline my father was working to instill.

"Love," my mother said. "This is what life is about."

"Do you love Dad?" I asked.

My mother looked away. She was strikingly beautiful, even at thirty-eight, and the men in our neighborhood said, when she was in school, that her beauty was such that men would bend to her every demand. Her dark hair, her pale skin, her big blue eyes: they had the effect of making her look both stunning and unapproachable.

My mother and father married when they were eighteen. I

was born two years later. My father joined the military the year before I was born and was gone, off and on, for the first six years of my life, beginning with boot camp and then the First Gulf War.

"He was so handsome in that uniform," my mother said, as if she could picture him, at age twenty-five, returning home from the war to be with us. A young couple walked by us on the way to their table. My mother blinked rapidly like something was caught in her eyes.

I was tall like my father, had the same dark hair and brown eyes, the same athletic build. My mother often said I was as handsome as my father but had gotten nothing of her beauty. "Look at you," she said. "You are so your father's son."

We sat there for a few minutes in silence. I was thinking about that, about what it meant to be my father's son. I knew she meant I looked like him, but I wondered if she knew something about me in that moment that I had yet to realize about myself.

My mother wiped her mouth with her napkin. She folded it into a neat little triangle and looked up at me. "How could I have known what kind of father he would be?" she asked, but I sensed that the question was not intended for me.

"Those early years without him," my mother said. "That was when I missed him and loved him most."

"Yeah," I said.

My mother looked right at me. "Don't be afraid to fall in love, Tully," she said. "At least your father and I can say we had that."

★ ★ ★

My mother was coming unhinged. The years of structure had driven her slightly mad. Our dinner should have been the first clue, but I didn't fully appreciate the changes until they became more obvious. With each passing month, my mother was trying her hand at new freedoms. At first it was more dinners out with me. But then there were other things. She stopped packing my lunch and handed me $10 bills when I left for school.

"Eat good," she said. "It's on your father."

By then she had quit her job and stayed home full time. She gave up all of her domestic duties, instead returning to sleep after she drove me to school, waking at noon to chain-smoke and watch soap operas and then Oprah. My mother would talk to me all through supper, which had become frozen pizzas or microwave dinners, about the characters in her shows and what was transpiring in their lives. For those first few months, my mother's life came to revolve around me being the only man in it.

★ ★ ★

My father's absence was a chance for me to be a kid. I did, as my mother had, let go of the chores and routines my father had begun to ingrain in me. I started to dream about a different future, one where I was a superstar athlete or a doctor or even a janitor. The point was, in these lives, my job had nothing to do with the military.

That being said, my status in the neighborhood and the lunchroom at school depended heavily on my father. In April, when Baghdad fell, news footage of the city played in the cafeteria. I remember the video of American soldiers taking down a statue of Saddam Hussein and I remember the way people came up and clapped me on the back or shook my hand. It was almost like I was a soldier and my classmates were paying homage to my service.

On the east side of the city, where we lived, no other fathers were military men. Some had been drafted into Vietnam, but none of them considered it a lifestyle. Those men were at least a decade or two older than my father. Those who hadn't served were slightly younger, in their early to mid-forties, but they were still older than my father and none of them would be fighting in this war. Most of the men in our neighborhood were blue-collar men, working at the brewery or fixing machines at the rail yard. Many of them didn't even have jobs as good as that. Maybe because so many of them might one day join the military, or because their fathers' lacked war stories, all of the guys in my neighborhood were hungry for mine. And, in this way, my father became a kind of legend, the way I spun him.

Before he left, my father had been respected. He was a kind neighbor, though people were uncomfortable around him because of his clean-cut look and reserved manner. He didn't participate in any of the neighborhood activities: barbequing, watching Buckeye games, or the neighborhood watch. Instead, he came and went from our house as if it were a military outpost, a place he would visit for R&R between battles or diplomatic engagements.

This, his mysterious lack of presence, was what I cashed in on. I described my father as the consummate solider, which he was, having come from a long line of men who had gone off to war and come back whole. He believed in his country. He believed in war. Above all else, he was a man who lived his life without fear. All of this was true. But the war stories I told, the letters I claimed he wrote, all of that was the stuff of my imagination. At night, when I was left without school to preoccupy me, I'd sit, watching CNN and NBC, hoping to catch a glimpse of my father in action.

I told tales of him during the invasion, flying over Iraq in a fighter jet, of him leading heavy artillery into prolonged battles. And once we'd taken the city, I spun new tales. "My father is taking a special forces unit deep into enemy territory," I told a lunch table full of freshmen girls. "They're hunting high-level officials and secret operatives. I'm going to sign up as soon as I turn eighteen. I'm going to fight right beside my father."

I'd even convinced the girl I had a crush on, Emma Brooks, during gym class, when we were square dancing, that my father was on his own special assignment, sitting in a foxhole on the outskirts of Baghdad, waiting for his chance to assassinate Saddam Hussein. "He taught me how to shoot," I told her. "He's going to end this war once and for all."

Though I'd been a fairly popular kid, handsome and clean-cut, athletic because of the training my father had put me through, I found the circle of people around me growing with every week that the war carried on, with every month that my father was gone.

★ ★ ★

On May 1 of that year, President George W. Bush gave a speech on an aircraft carrier that was televised on every major news channel. I sat, just over a month left in school, hoping he would offer me something worthwhile to bring to my classmates, and in a way he did, though at the same time he got me asking serious questions about my father that I had never thought to ask before.

That day, standing in front of a crowd of servicemen and -women, the president declared "mission accomplished" in Iraq. I knew then that the next day at school would be a kind of hero's welcome for me. People would be happy for me, happy for my father, they would think that we had won the war and that my father must be coming home.

My mother and I hadn't heard from my father since he had left for the war, which, by May 1, meant we'd gone two months without any news. This worried me. If the war had been won, then where was my father, why hadn't he tried to contact us to share the good news?

★ ★ ★

"The funny thing about war," my father once told me, "is that there is nothing predictable about it." That didn't strike me as particularly profound until two weeks after the president's declaration of victory, when a military man knocked on our door to inform my mother that her husband had gone MIA.

For days I read and reread the letter, trying to understand it, searching it for a story that could fill the void that was just now opening in me. I carried the letter in the back pocket of my jeans, and at school I would read it every half-hour, searching for some new detail to make it make sense. I couldn't, remembering the disciplined man who'd left us, imagine my father being lost. It didn't seem like something he was capable of.

The next day at school I told a few of my friends, and before the day was out everyone knew. Emma Brooks came up and hugged me, and though I missed my father immensely just then, I was happy to have her holding me. I was happy, in the coming weeks, because she stayed close to me, perhaps sensing that I needed her.

The rest of the school year was like that. People were, and it is the only word I can think to describe it, tender toward me. By then I'd told dozens of stories about my father and his heroics. Everyone, in the last weeks of school, was in mourning, and for this reason I was almost glad when the summer hit.

★ ★ ★

For the months of June and July my mother mourned our loss, treating my father's MIA status more like a KIA. For days on end she would cry and then suddenly come out of it, declaring her hatred for him, her happiness that he was gone and she was forever free.

"Where did all that disciple get him?" she said. "Nowhere but dead, gone. All those push-ups and sit-ups, the running around in the backyard, none of it any good."

My mother lived in her room, curtains drawn, empty bottles of Seagram's and 7 Up scattered about in small piles. I would go to comfort her, sharing the food I'd prepared or bringing her a new box of tissues. Sometimes we would lie together in her bed and watch old movies. Other times the door would be locked and she would ask me to leave her alone or she wouldn't answer at all.

Throughout the summer, while my mother was locked inside, I would be on the streets with my friends, playing baseball or listening to the radio, smoking cigarettes on someone's front porch. There, in the heat of June and July, we would speculate aloud about my father and where he had disappeared to. My friends had sort of adopted him because of the stories I'd told and because, I think, they sensed my growing worry.

"I don't believe he's lost," they said. "Probably on some secret mission, kind of shit the government has to keep way under wraps."

"I bet it's something like that," I said.

"Or maybe he has Bin Laden and Hussein in custody and he is interrogating them right now, getting them to reveal the next terror plot," they said. They talked torture techniques and made up long-winded confessions.

This was how it went all summer. We'd talk through different scenarios, pinpoint my father's mission, his location, the people he was with, and the reasons why we had to be lied to about his whereabouts. And in this way it felt, at least for a while, like nothing had changed.

★ ★ ★

In September, just before I went back to school, my mother started seeing another man. I wasn't prepared for this. Her sister, who was a secretary at Ohio State, had set them up. My aunt thought it would be good for my mother to get out of the house and be chased by a man.

His name was Neil. He was what my father would have called a "Flaming Liberal" or a "New Age Hippie." He was into protesting the Iraq War and the Bush administration, and he claimed to be a feminist, though I was pretty sure he only said that so he could get laid.

Neil had an extensive record collection. Every day in September he would bring more and more of his records to our house. One night, he took me down to the basement, where he had set up my father's record player, and played me his favorite one.

"See," he said, "this is Jimi Hendrix. He's playing at Woodstock."

Neil talked to me like I was a little kid.

"I think I've heard of it," I said, trying to be a smart ass.

"Of course," he said. "I'm just saying is all."

We stood there, two boys really, listening to Jimi play. I knew Neil liked it because he thought it meant something about overcoming "Big Brother" and about ending war, which it did. But to me it was about more than that, it was about a deep oppression that Neil knew nothing about, something he could never learn or understand. I only knew it because I lived in a neighborhood that still dealt with it. Most of the boys I'd told war stories to were going to go off to war soon, not because they wanted to or because their fathers were making them, but because this was what the world had made them for. They didn't have the privilege to say no. There weren't that many jobs to be had without a college education, and most of them weren't going to go to college. They were blue-collar kids who wanted to stay blue-collar. They really didn't have that many options. This was, in fact, why my father stayed here and did not move us to a suburb. "These are the men you will be serving with," he said. "These are the men we send off to die in our wars."

That night in the basement, I was thinking about this, about the difference between the boys fighting in this war and the ones, like Neil, who were protesting it.

"What do you think?" Neil asked when the song ended and the record stopped.

"Pretty cool," I said. "I think he really hit it on the head."

"You're not messing with me, are you?" Neil asked.

I looked at him then for a long second. I wanted to be mean, to say the things any boy would want to say when a new man had come to replace his father in his mother's heart, but I didn't have it in me. Neil was good to my mother. He was affectionate in ways my father had never been, touching her face and hugging her and calling her pet names. On the one hand it made me sick, but on the other it made me happy for my mother. She was smart and interesting and beautiful. She deserved to be shown some attention.

"No, man," I said. "It's a really good song."

When my father left I didn't miss him. I was certain he would return. Now, with his disappearance lasting indefinitely and with my mother seeing another man, I yearned for his rules, for his uniform and clean-cut hair. In this way I began to miss my father's discipline, began to long for it.

That night, after Neil played me his record, I took my father's clippers and shaved my head clean down to the scalp. I laid out my clothes for the next morning and set the alarm for 0700 so I could shower and make the bed. The next day was the start of school.

★ ★ ★

Across the whole of September and into October, I would return home on weekdays to do push-ups and sit-ups on the living room floor while I watched CNN and C-SPAN, following the war closely, hoping that there might be news of my father. On the weekends, I spent my time doing the chores my father and I would have done. I raked the leaves, painted the shed and fence, and covered the air-conditioning units. I did everything I could to avoid my mother and Neil and to keep telling myself that my father was coming home. I stayed late at school or spent my time near the river fishing.

At school, I tried my best to stay focused, to stay optimistic. Most people avoided me now, whereas before they had wanted stories. Who could blame them? Time was passing and their lives were moving forward toward graduation. The war looked more and more like a long-term thing.

★ ★ ★

During Halloween that year, my school held a haunted house for charity. We could go and pay a quarter to bob for apples or to have our fortune read, or pay a dollar to go into the haunted house.

There I saw Emma Brooks. I hadn't seen her much over the summer, but since school had started back, we'd been hanging out again. She had long dark hair and a small frame, "like a baby bird," my mother said when I pointed her out once. Emma was working as a fortuneteller. She had put on a black dress and dark makeup. She wore a ring on every finger. I walked up to her and laid my hand on her crystal ball, running my palm over the smooth cold surface of it.

"Hey, Tully," she said. "What are you supposed to be?"

"Just me," I said. "I actually only came to see you."

Emma blushed. I had never been so forward with her, even after my mother suggested I ask her on a date, saying, "It will be my treat. You can take her anywhere." But I never asked. Emma and I were friends and I was afraid to ruin that.

"I need you to tell me something," I said.

The hallway where Emma had her booth was quiet. She had wanted it this way, saying that she couldn't concentrate on answers with a lot of noise.

"What can I do for you?" she asked.

It wasn't that most people had forgotten about my father by then. They hadn't, but I talked less about him, and it had been almost five months since that letter had arrived. I wasn't shocked that Emma hadn't seen this coming, but it made me a little sad, too.

"Will my father come home?" I asked.

Emma reached her hand across the table and laid it on top of mine, the one that was rubbing the crystal ball. Her skin felt warm. It reminded me of the cookies my mother would bake when my father was still home. I could tell by the way she laid it there, in that delicate way, that Emma didn't want to answer the question.

"I need to know," I said.

She looked up at me then. She had this pained expression on her face, kind of like when someone winces, but it looked more thoughtful somehow. I imagined, looking at her big dark eyes, that she knew the answer, but I sensed that she was about to tell me what she thought I wanted to hear instead of the truth. I knew, though, I could see it in the initial expression, that the answer was no, that she thought my father was never coming home again.

I looked away for a second, blinking back tears.

I drew in a deep, hard breath.

"He'll be back, Tully," she said, squeezing my hand. "I promise."

I looked at Emma and her eyes were really wet, the way I imagined mine might be just then. I leaned toward her, squeezing her hand. I kissed her, for the first time, pressing my lips against hers and closing my eyes. I stayed there for just a few seconds. It felt like the right amount of time. Then I stepped back, letting go of her hand.

"Thank you," I said, and I turned to walk away.

★ ★ ★

That night, I went home and strung up Christmas lights in the backyard. I worked feverishly, pulling them from the storage totes in the basement and stringing them haphazardly around the edges of the obstacle course. I was sure I needed to start training on the course again, that this is what my father would have wanted in his absence.

When I was done with the lights, I went down and retrieved my father's record player and one of Neil's old records, the one he'd played for me with Jimi Hendrix doing "The Star Spangled Banner" at Woodstock. I set them where my father had when we were running drills, and I turned the volume all the way up. I stripped down to my underwear. Jimi struck that first chord and I began to run.

Jimi was halfway into his rendition when Neil came out. He was in flannel pajamas, wearing a pair of my mother's slippers. I had just completed my first pass through the course.

"Tully, what are you doing?" Neil asked. "It's 1 a.m."

I stopped and walked over toward him. He was a short man with shaggy hair, a fluffy beard, and a pair of horn-rimmed glasses. He looked like a man who knew nothing about war.

"Jesus," he said. "You must be freezing."

174

Neil was not a bad man and I had no real hate for him. He was not my father. That was his only crime.

"0100 hours," I said.

"What?"

"You said 1 a.m. It's 0100 hours."

Neil looked at me with a confused expression, his eyes narrowing and the skin on his forehead wrinkling. "Seriously, Tully, we've got to get you inside."

That was what did it, I think. His concern. Or maybe it was his fingers touching my elbow and my thinking that not so long ago those same fingers had been touching my mother. My own father had never laid a kind hand on me, and maybe in the end that is why things came apart the way they did. I guess I'll never be sure, but in that instant, when Neil's flesh pressed up against mine, all I could think to do was to start asking questions. I wanted to beat the piss out of him, drag him into the street and stomp him until he was tucked into the fetal position, crying and bleeding all over the road. But that wouldn't have given me the answers I so desperately needed.

Neil looked at me, almost like he was pleading, like he sensed something in me was about to come unglued. He started to guide me inside by my elbow, as if I were some kind of child who was lost.

I pulled my arm away very gently. I stood there looking him in the eyes.

"Does she ever talk about him?" I asked.

Neil flinched. It was almost like I had thrown a punch.

"Tully?" he said.

"Does she ever talk about my father?" I said.

Neil reached out to touch me again, but I stepped back.

My mother appeared then.

"What's going on?" she said. Her robe was pulled tight around her, to ward off the cold. "Tully, what's wrong?"

A wave of relief came over Neil's face. He was not going to have to answer my question.

My mother walked toward us, and as she came I sat down very slowly.

Neil and my mother exchanged a glance and then he walked away, leaving us alone. She bent to sit with me in the grass, our shadows blinking on and off with the Christmas lights.

"He isn't coming back, is he?" I asked.

My mother reached for me.

"You don't have to lie to me," I said.

She pressed my face into her shoulder.

"He isn't," she said.

In the morning, I woke up and went to the local recruitment office where my father once worked. I enlisted. Through the winter and into the spring I trained, running that obstacle course like my father had taught me, adhering to the tenets of discipline that he'd set out to show me. In June, just before I went off to basic, we got news that he was dead. Then, I went off to war.

But that night, sitting in our backyard, with my head in my mother's lap, with the Christmas lights blinking—one, two, three, one, two, three, one, like soldiers marching—Jimi Hendrix reached the part, right at the end of the song, where he's holding that last distorted chord, stretching it out like it might go on forever. But it didn't go on forever. The record ended, and everything went silent.

—